Ex Libris
St. Mary of the Springs
College
Columbus, Ohio

The
SEED IS BLOWN

by ALICE WRIGHT

Illustrated by Joan Berg

RAND McNALLY & COMPANY
CHICAGO · NEW YORK · SAN FRANCISCO

CHAPTER ONE

"*Chicot! Chicot!* The teeth of the river!" Josiah Lake shouted, from the bow of the deck, the French boatman's alarm of a snag ahead.

From his pilot stand on the cabin roof of the boat, Winthrop, startled, saw the fallen sycamore downstream under the Ohio's green surface.

"Bear to your right!" Josiah called, raising the metal-tipped setting pole and leaning forward to jab at the rising and falling boughs of the driftwood.

Winthrop did not take time to determine if it was a floating sawyer adrift with the current or a planter now firmly rooted in the river bottom. All he knew was that the claw-like boughs could rip apart the stoutest vessel. He leaned sharply against the long steersman's oar, pitting all his strength and will against the stubborn craft until at last it turned slowly, barely scraping past a reaching limb, and left the snag astern.

He drew a deep breath. That was too close! He hadn't been tending his turn at steering as he should, especially since he and his father were the only manpower on the boat. His sisters Suzanne and Merry were of no help what-ever in piloting a boat through the whirlpools and currents, past sandbars, out of the way of the great commercial keel-

54256

boats, or in avoiding being dashed against a rocky bank by the treacherous Ohio.

Suzanne, he admitted grudgingly, was a passing good cook, but little Merry was worse than a frolicsome pup underfoot and wailed every time he tied her with a rope to keep her from falling overboard. He was glad both were securely inside the cabin now, asleep, he hoped, among the cargo of grist from their own mills.

Josiah flung the setting pole to the deck. "Mind your task, son, if we're to reach Kentucky!"

"Yes, sir," Winthrop answered, stung by his father's rare fit of anger. He wondered rebelliously why they were going to the Kentucky country anyway. The Lake cabin back home in Pennsylvania let in hardly a draft in winter. In spring, the air was sweet with the scent of the apple tree by the stable and the honeysuckle spilling over the rail fence.

It couldn't be that his father—like most with the fever for making a cornpatch or tomahawk claim in Kentucky— wanted to farm the land, because Josiah was a miller, and a good one, to whom families from all over Ligonier Valley had brought their grain. Winthrop studied him with mingled pride and anxiety. A small, dark man, he was, quietly dressed in his butternut-dyed shirt, sober homespun breeches, and good boots; clean-shaven; his long black hair tied neatly back. He seemed out of place against the wild river background, except for the powder horn slung from one shoulder, the bullet pouch at his belt, and the wide hat pulled low against the July sun.

It was six, or was it seven, days since they had left

6

Fort Pitt? There had been delays, of course: for getting supplies in Wheeling; for leisurely breakfasts ashore in the morn-
ings; for spending one afternoon shifting the cargo. Another
afternoon had passed when they tied up alongside a migrant
farm family whose floating box had presented itself in such
a comical way. With each change of wind or current, the
box had offered front, side, and end views of its contents—
chickens, cows, hay, vegetables, farm tools, furniture, and
the family. The Lakes found the temptation to visit too
great to be resisted.

By comparison, Winthrop thought, the Lake craft had
neat, Kentucky-boat style. Each timber had been selected
with an eye to its usefulness in building a new home. In fact,
the boat *was* part of home. The heavy upright beams of the
cabin once supported the great millwheel. The watertight
bottom was caulked together from the mill's siding. Although she was square instead of curved at bow and stern,
like the great commercial boats, and though she had no
need of sidewalks for a rowing or poling crew, the length
was a good thirty feet, the breadth ten. The cabin roof was
shingled. She rode about four feet above water and was
held together by over a thousand white-oak pins. Through
the long winter evenings Josiah and Winthrop had whittled
them—five inches long, head one inch square, tapered at
the peg—until both could turn them out without looking.
Winthrop had decorated the prow with a set of antlers, and
had carved over the cabin door: FOR KENTUCKY, JULY
1788. Josiah had put finishing touches to the doorway by
building over it a bracket for his musket.

Winthrop noticed that his father was covering with a

large tarred canvas the deck cargo of barrels of lard and kegs of pickled pork. He squinted at the sky and saw the gunsmoke-blue haze over the eastern ridge. "Think a squall's blowing up?" he asked, setting the oar and clambering down the short ladder.

"Probably won't break until nightfall, but we'd best start looking for a place to moor," Josiah answered. "We'll head for shore and shelter below the first point of land we come to." Josiah again slipped away into his own thoughts.

It was easy to see by the look of listening and waiting upon his face that he was already way off yonder in his mind, where Winthrop could never follow. Now that time had eased his own grief over his mother's death, it was clear as noonday to Winthrop that she would say, "Feather up!" to any pining. He pictured her, small and gay, turning the handle of her music box and humming a French tune. Maybe that was what his father kept listening and waiting for.

Winthrop, without intention, stumbled against a cask and set it rolling.

"Take care not to wake your sisters," Josiah cautioned. "Merry has hardly napped since we left the Ligonier, and even Suzanne slept fitfully last night."

Lack of sleep could not put a damper on Merry's baby prankishness, but Suzanne did need rest. The shadows under her blue eyes showed that. Poor Suzanne! She was terrified of the wilderness and the big river. Winthrop must be careful lest his own uneasiness show. Just now, when she was not around for him to set an example for, he could sound out his father on questions that were troubling him.

Leaning against the cabin, he put on an air of casual-

8

ness. "With the Tories licked and the Indians brought to treaty, this country should be peaceable as a meetinghouse on the Sabbath."

Josiah secured a corner of the canvas to the gunwale before he straightened and turned to him. Winthrop felt his father's look of appraisal travel from bare feet, buckskin breeches, naked torso, past the kerchief knotted about his head. "Nobody'd guess you were reared in civilization long as you'd keep such notions to yourself," Josiah said with a slow smile. "No, Winthrop. The British aren't licked now, and the Indians are still foes to be reckoned with around here."

"The British aren't licked?" Winthrop echoed incredulously. "Everyone knows we trounced them seven years ago."

"Yes," Josiah admitted, taking the tar bucket from a peg and handing it to Winthrop. "Weight the canvas where it bellies. We won the war for independence," he continued, "but the British still have their trading posts. A mighty inviting section this is, we're passing through." His gaze narrowed. "A rich source of game and fur, a plum for land speculators, a military wedge into the East or West."

Winthrop looked around him. All he could see was the wide river leading endlessly into more and more dismal forest. It didn't look very inviting to him.

Josiah's eyes began to twinkle. "Too wild for your taste?"

Winthrop almost dropped the tar bucket in his surprise. Josiah must have read his mind! What was more, he seemed to be coming out of his long aloofness. Caring less for the answer than the chance to keep him from closing up again, Winthrop asked, "Suppose the forests are crawling with Lobster Backs right now?"

"You'll not catch sight of one, leastways not one in the British redcoat uniform," declared Josiah. He lowered his voice. "At the Indian council fires from Shawneetown to the Maumee there are British agents posing as traders and whipping to a fever pitch their natural hatred of the intruding settlers."

Winthrop sought for the twinkle again, but seeing that Josiah was in earnest, he dropped all pretense. "I heard that just two weeks ago a band of Shawnees ambushed a settler Kentucky bound. They cut off his ears, shot him black with powder, made him walk over hot coals while squaws beat him with clubs and poked him with fiery sticks, and scalped him while he was still alive."

Josiah's face went still. "Wherever did you hear such a tale?"

"Back at Simeral's Ferry. A French Canadian voyageur up from Vincennes told me."

"Such talk is strong for a boy not yet sixteen," muttered Josiah. "I'm sorry you heard it. I hope there's little truth to it. But since you did hear it, let's look at the situation fair and square." He paced the small clearing on the deck as he explained.

"The Indians set great store by friendship. They've been taught to look on us as traitors to our king and our race. But they have been friendly with the British ever since the first traders packed over the mountains or down from the lake trails to buy pelts and pass out free rum and ammunition. A fine arrangement—furs at a fraction of their value, warriors to use against the colonists."

Winthrop swallowed hard. "And now against us!" Frowning, he tried to puzzle it out. "I thought the treaties made us friends. Take the Shawnees. Two years ago, they gave up claim to the Ohio valley. Now, they're hopping mad because settlers are moving in."

"It's one thing to be agreeable to half-understood promises written on paper, another to be driven from your homeland," Josiah said thoughtfully. "Besides, Little Turtle says the treaty at Fort Finney was signed by delegates who had no sanction from their principal chiefs." He smiled sadly. "The Shawnees have cause not to respect our treaties, you know. Chief Cornstalk was murdered at Point Pleasant when he came to council in good faith. All the relatives of Mingo Chief Logan, even his women and children, were shot, tomahawked, and stabbed in cold blood. Then there was the massacre of the Christian Moravian Indians—"

"I see." Winthrop whistled softly. "From their point of view, they have reason to cut up lone settlers and burn them bit by bit—" His voice trailed off.

Suzanne stood frozen in the doorway. In her rigid hands she held a small wooden bowl. Winthrop and Josiah stared, first at the girl, then solemnly at each other. How much had she heard?

Josiah went quickly toward her and put out a hand to touch her shoulder. "Bless my soul! You look a picture in that blue frock!"

So she did, thought Winthrop. A picture of a girl drawn taut as a bowstring with fright.

11

Suzanne stood frozen in the doorway

Josiah took from her uplifted bowl the flat round of cornbread. "Journey cake—johnnycake—whatever any' body wants to call it, it's good! And just what I've been hankering for." He remembered she had baked it on the smooth, flat journey-board that was propped against last night's roaring supper blaze on the Federal (Virginia) shore, while Winthrop had made fast the boat for the night and set a line over the side, hopeful of pulling up a fish for break' fast. "Come, Suzanne, you sit right here." He led her to an overturned keg and made himself a seat beside her. "Winthrop, fetch a gourd of that good spring water from the cask."

There was a stretch of clear, smooth river ahead—a calm before the storm, perhaps—so they could let their craft drift for a little. Comforting Suzanne was the impor' tant thing at the moment.

Suzanne sat obediently on the keg. At last she managed to ask through stiff lips, "Will they burn us bit by bit, too?"

Winthrop turned from the water cask, gourd dipper poised. Josiah's hands tightened on the bowl. A shadow of defeat settled over him, then lifted slowly as he looked into Suzanne's upturned face. "Never you mind. No harm shall come to us." He gestured to the wilderness about them. "It's not all like this. Soon—perhaps tomorrow, even—we'll visit the New Englanders' settlement at the mouth of the Muskingum, and you'll see. There's no handsomer pile of buildings west of the Allegheny Mountains than the dwell' ings General Rufus Putnam is building there. Meant to house fifty or sixty families."

"Fort Harmar is just a few rods away, on the west side

of the Muskingum," Winthrop added, with a heartiness he hoped was convincing.

"And across the Ohio, on the Virginia side, a Pennsylvanian by the name of Isaac Williams has turned the bottomlands into a plantation. Remember Mr. Zane's plantation, on the big island by Wheeling? It would be like that. We'll trade with him for the makings of a feast, eh?"

Winthrop made himself comfortable on the deck floor. Watching Suzanne, he saw the look of fear ebb from her face as her father talked quietly of the morrow. He stretched, relaxed. Then suddenly he sat bolt upright, trying to trace the sound that fell softly, brokenly on the air. Was it the tinkle of a music box? No. His imagination was playing tricks. Seeing Josiah take hold again had stirred his fancy until it seemed his pretty French mother was close, too.

The faint tinkle again—from the direction of the cabin! It must be, it could only be Merry playing Mamma's music box. But that had been forbidden for months! Winthrop glanced quickly at Suzanne. Her gaze was fastened to the square toes of her shoes, and a tell-tale flush spread from her throat into her cheeks.

"Father told you to leave it home," Winthrop accused her, for the moment forgetting Josiah's presence.

Suzanne's head came up with a sudden jerk that sent her yellow braids swinging. Her blue eyes flashed defiantly. "It would have been wrong to leave without one thing Mamma loved."

Winthrop was too taken aback by her show of spirit and by the enormity of what she had done to speak.

Josiah sat stark still. Finally he rose, took off his hat,

"Pretty?" She held up the music box

threw it aside, and gazed back up the long reach of river. "At home there was everything to remind me I had lost her."

"So that's why we left, why you told me not to bring her music box?" A note of sympathy crept into Suzanne's voice.

"Yes," Josiah answered stonily. "Come out, Merry!"

Winthrop and Suzanne scarcely dared to breathe as Merry slipped out of the doorway. Her short copper curls shook in the breeze and the light trembling on the now ruffling water reflected over her face like laughter. More than ever she was the elfin image of her mother. "Pretty?" She held up the music box for all to see.

"Play it, child," Josiah commanded.

"Like this?" Merry turned the handle experimentally. Note by note, clumsily, the tune was played.

"Bring it to me," Josiah said quietly. He bent to lift the music box from her small outstretched arms. One hand stroked the carved lid, hesitated over the ivory handle, then turned it smoothly. "Like this."

A smile of delight spread over Merry's face as the melody spun out warm and as full of grace as sunlight moving over tall grass. "Sing!" she cried, pointing an imperious finger at her father.

Josiah appeared to wait for the refrain, then began:

The seed is blown before the wind
And where it comes to rest . . .

Winthrop tried to take up the next lines, but he could not remember the words.

Josiah suddenly set aside the music box. There was a long silence while he again stared upriver. Then his face eased as if someone had smoothed away the look of listening and waiting with gentle finger tips. He turned, and slowly his smile encompassed Winthrop, whose answering smile glowed eagerly; Suzanne, whose level gaze read the gratitude he could not speak; and Merry, who dimpled at him as she curiously poked a finger under the lid of the music box. There was a new lift to Josiah's shoulders as if he had heard Mamma's "Feather up!" in the silence.

"Well, now, since we're together, each to his task before our cargo and ourselves are drenched. I haven't seen a good place to tie up. We may as well ride out the storm."

Merry snatched up the music box, hugging it, and raced for the cabin. "I keep it dry!" she promised.

16

"Be careful you don't drop it!" Suzanne scooped the dipper and bowl from the deck and hurried after her.

They were hardly below, when a gun shot suddenly cracked faintly across the water, the direction from which it came uncertain. Winthrop straightened up and listened. His eyes scanned empty shorelines and dark walls of forest. "What was it? And where?"

"Hush," Josiah whispered. "Don't alarm the children. Probably just a hunter."

Winthrop noticed that nevertheless Josiah snatched his musket from the bracket over the cabin door.

"Look!" Winthrop pointed across the river to a canoe that broke from the green forest wall as if by magic. It must have come through a creek mouth concealed by overhanging trees that bordered the Indian wilderness shore. The two men, bending lustily to the paddles, might be trappers, since pelts were heaped in the center of the canoe.

In another instant the reason for their haste was apparent. With blood-chilling yells three Indians parted the willows on the bank above the creek mouth, leaped into the shallows, and waded waist-deep, in hot pursuit of the canoe. The half-naked warrior in the lead was fitting an arrow into his great bow.

"Get down!" Josiah pulled Winthrop to his side on the deck. "Don't lift your head!" he panted.

Against his father's advice, Winthrop peered warily over the lard cask. His mouth fell open as he saw the man at the stern paddle, an arrow in his breast, pitch backward into the river.

A shot from the lone trapper barked out. The lead

Indian dropped his bow, clawed at his throat, then flailed convulsively in the water. The other warriors paused to drag their injured comrade ashore. The trapper turned and paddled furiously downstream. His cry for help floated eerily on the wind.

Winthrop sank back on his heels, trembling and wordless as his father handed him the powder horn.

"Pour me a measure." Josiah spoke hurriedly while he fumbled in the pouch at his belt for bullets and began to load his musket. "I can't leave that man without aid. You understand?" He paused to look searchingly at Winthrop.

Satisfied, he went on. "You know how to handle the boat. Suzanne may have to help. The current is running better than four miles an hour now. Keep Merry inside. Bear mid-river and travel all night. You should reach Putnam's settlement tomorrow forenoon. Wait there for me."

He inched toward the stern and pulled their small trailing dugout canoe close.

Winthrop scrambled after Josiah. It was one thing to be afraid, another to be a coward!

Josiah, about to step into the canoe, turned and in one swift movement pushed Winthrop to the floor. With a soft thud an arrow buried its head into the cask near his hand and quivered there. Shocked into silence, Winthrop watched the summer-warm lard ooze out between his fingers.

Josiah dropped into the dugout, now swaying restlessly alongside. Swiftly he cut its towline rather than take time to untie. "Don't waste a minute getting away from this area!" he ordered.

"We'll go down a way, then hold up and wait for you."

Winthrop rose and called in despair as the current caught his craft broadside and the distance between him and his father lengthened.

"No! Keep on! Get out of sight on the Federal side, beyond that island tip. I'll join you at the settlement. Take care of your sisters!" Across the widening water space, Josiah's command rang clear.

As Winthrop turned to his task at the steering oar, something bit into his palm. The powder horn cap! He must have been clutching it ever since he measured out the powder. Now it was bent, and a jagged bit of the horn neck was attached to it. Instead of unscrewing the cap, he must have broken it off in his haste and excitement, he thought vaguely. Now he tucked it into his breeches pocket.

Safe around the island tip, he could better view the menace of the darkening storm clouds. The heavy, soundless tumult and pressure of them was akin to a force deepening within himself, one that demanded release in tears. For a moment he closed his eyes tightly, blocking them back. Next moment, a streak of lightning with a clap of thunder at its heels splintered the air and his tears were forgotten. A sudden gust rippled along the shore, bending the trees into waves that tossed off sprays of frightened birds. Rain began moving across the water like a huge curtain closing away the rest of the world.

Suzanne crept out.

"Get back inside!" Winthrop shouted.

She stood her ground. "Father said I should help."

Winthrop grudgingly turned over to her the long steering oar.

"We aim to steer and stay midstream for a while." To himself he added, "Out of bowshot." And he took up his stand with the sharp-pointed setting pole warding off threat-ening snags and planters.

When the worst of the sultry thunderstorm was over, rain continued to fall. Each lift and thrust of his pole be-came a torment to Winthrop's arms; his whole body ached with fatigue as he tried to keep footing on the slippery boat planks. The long night lay ahead with its treacherous snags, sandbars, and riffles; there was the constant sense of hostile eyes watching him from shore. There was anxiety about his father. How might Josiah have fared in the storm, on his errand of mercy in their little dugout canoe? There was a nearer, deeper anxiety, too. He peered at Suzanne as she huddled over the great steering oar, half protected by a tarpaulin to be sure, but shivering in the dismal down-pour. No amount of wheedling or threatening had persuaded her to leave her post.

It was Merry's thin wail, growing louder and more protesting in the cabin, that finally drew her inside. Win-throp listened awhile to Suzanne's comforting voice and the faint tinkle of the music box, then turned his full attention to guiding the boat through the darkness.

As the night wore on, Winthrop came to be grateful for the sheet lightning that flickered over the river. Its hard glare etched, with unearthly clarity, snatches of the course ahead. One after another the impressions came in nightmare parade until, during a long pause, he sat down to flex his aching feet and rub his tired thighs. His head nodded, fell against his knees, and he slept.

He woke to a clap of thunder and Suzanne calling his name and warning. "Winthrop! We're heading inshore! Here, let me—"

"Yes, Susu." Drowsily he rose, shook her off, shook himself awake, and pulled at the long oar-sweep in time to avoid the bank.

"Merry?"

"Asleep on the feather tick between the crates."

"You go back and get some more rest. I can manage." He hoped he sounded more confident than he felt.

"No." The touch of Suzanne's hand was warm and oddly welcome. "Here, we can share this tarpaulin. It's big enough to cover us both."

Winthrop groped his way to her side. Both, with a hand on the long oar, looked intently ahead. An owl whooped somewhere along the shore. The answer that quavered back seemed to come from a point right at their side. Not even a screechowl would be flying midstream in a storm! Winthrop straightened, every sense alert. Dimly he made out a long object to starboard. A driftlog? No! It was a slender birch canoe! In it a dark figure moved rhythmically. Winthrop reached back to muffle Suzanne's gasp, dropped silently to the deck roof and cautiously peered over. A sudden glare of lightning! Too late to draw back, he found himself staring into the face of an Indian who was gazing searchingly at him. The face burned itself deep into Winthrop's memory. The instant was gone and all was darkness. He lay still while the canoe passed, gliding silently on in the night.

21

CHAPTER TWO

The following morning, heavy-eyed, stiff-muscled, and wet, Winthrop stretched on his back to rest in the sun that was warming the cabin roof. Suzanne spread the canvas to dry, unplaited her hair, and shook it loose in the freshening wind.

"I'll never forget that Indian's face!" She shuddered as she spoke.

"He could have shot us like sitting ducks if he meant us harm," Winthrop reminded her. His own impression he kept to himself.

Suzanne looked toward the forest. The warm sunshine seemed to stop short of the somber green.

"It's a friendlier place than it looks to be," he said, knowing the girl's fear of the wilderness.

Suzanne glanced over her shoulder and nodded. "At least one can take cover in it."

"There's game, and firewood to cook it with; ripe berries in the thicket, and springs to drink from. There probably are no regular trails to follow, but a man could walk the distance from the creek mouth to the Muskingum faster than we're managing," he suggested.

Suzanne's face brightened with hope. "You mean Father might have found his way through the forest and be waiting for us at the settlement?"

"It's possible. If he isn't there when we arrive, we'll go to General Rufus Putnam."

Suzanne looked in dismay at her bedraggled skirts, and at Winthrop's matted hair and sodden clothing. "Go over-side and bathe. There are dry breeches in the wood chest."

Winthrop eyed the muddy rain-swollen river with dis-taste. "I've had my fill of water," he grumbled. What was coming over the girl to be ordering him about woman-fash-ion? Nevertheless, with a quizzical glance back at Suzanne, he went below to change.

"What do we do now?" Merry asked as Winthrop, dry in neatly mended homespun, hoisted her to the roof deck.

"We watch for the sentry towers of a big fort where there are soldier men. Twice a day they parade with drums and fifes," he answered. "Perhaps we shall see and hear them."

"Is Papa there?" Merry turned pansy-soft eyes to Su-zanne.

Suzanne looked down at her and smiled. "Soon." She drew Merry gently to her and tied a short rope about her waist. Merry, sensing that something had gone wrong, for-got to protest.

As the morning wore on, it seemed that the river was moving only deeply inside, leaving the boat poised on its surface. Finally Winthrop discarded caution and turned toward the shallows off the Virginia shore. There at least he could push with the pole. Around this bend, and the next, surely beyond the long, crescent-shaped island, lay the settlement.

When the boat drifted past the island tip, it was

Merry who first caught sight of Fort Harmar, perched high on the right bank of the Ohio. "There is the soldiers' fort! There it is!"

"And that must be Isaac William's plantation!" Suzanne cried, pointing to the neatly laid fields on the Virginia bottomland on the left.

Winthrop swung his gaze from one landmark to the other. There must be no mistake. His heart beat faster as he watched the sentry tower above the bristling palisade loom nearer. He searched intently for the outlet of the river that would be the Muskingum. There it was, spewing driftwood from under a tunnel of trees overarching at the very foot of the fort.

Fort Harmar

On the east point opposite was a cluster of huts. Against the bank beneath them was a wharf fringed with river craft. He braced heavily on the steersman's oar and set for a tack across the channel toward it. Suzanne, trembling with excitement, helped Merry down the ladder. "More to the right!" she directed.

Winthrop set his feet wide, bent his head, and strained every muscle of his shoulders and back against the tiller-oar.

"Good! We're making straight for the landing!" Suzanne called.

At last Winthrop felt the pull of the current slacken, and looked up to see that the distance between the bow and shore was a mere three boat-lengths. A man came running down the bank, shouting and waving welcome. For a moment Winthrop sagged with relief. The thought of his father bolstered him and he jumped to the bow and threw the mooring line. The man seized it and hauled their proud Kentucky-bound craft up against the landing wharf.

"Hi! Where's the master here?" The tall young man's manner was scholarly, in contrast to his suit of soft-dressed deerskin.

"Hasn't he arrived yet?" Winthrop asked, his sense of foreboding deepening. "Josiah Lake is his name."

"Perhaps I may have a word with your mother?'

"My sisters and I—are alone," answered Winthrop.

The young man's intelligent eyes took in the situation. He strode aboard and swept Merry to his shoulders. "It is breakfast you're needing, my young miss." He bowed slightly toward Winthrop. "Welcome! Anselm Tupper at your service." Turning to Suzanne, he offered his hand to help

"Hasn't he arrived yet?" Winthrop asked

her over the gunwale. "Come ashore. It may be that General Putnam has word of your father."

Winthrop remembered his manners and introduced himself and his sisters before following them up the slippery bank. Looking about, as they reached the plain above the river, he thought that "Putnam's Paradise," as some called the new settlement at the Muskingum, was a sorry looking place indeed. The windows of the scattered huts were covered with oiled paper and there were no chimneys. The paths between them were stump-filled and muddy.

"So this is Rufus Putnam's settlement?" Winthrop hoped his polite tone masked his disappointment.

Anselm Tupper's mouth twitched humorously. "The

advance party, getting things ready for the families of the Ohio Company's founders, bunk here. We call this area The Point."

"Oh!" Winthrop spoke absently. "It will be some time before it's ready to house nine hundred people, won't it?"

"Indeed!" Anselm's eyebrows arched high, but pride and laughter were in his voice. "Did you think the general who designed the fortifications at West Point would own to such huts as these? Ah, no!" He waved toward a mass of trees on a higher plain, further up the Muskingum. "Rufus Putnam's Campus Martius is being built up there."

"Campus Martius?" The words came awkwardly to Suzanne's lips. "What does it mean?"

"Military Camp," he explained, grinning down at her. "A Field of War."

"But Father talked of a peaceable settlement," Suzanne murmured.

Anselm's gray eyes sobered. "And so it is. General Putnam and the members of the Ohio Company have talked much about the promise of life in this new country. On their word, some are already crossing the mountains."

"The idea of going into the wilderness under the direction of a company is strange to me," said Winthrop.

"It's really very simple; it's plain arithmetic," Anselm replied with a light shrug. "After the Revolutionary War, those who had done service were to be paid off in Continental money. As you probably know, it is of little value."

Suzanne nodded knowingly. "Often Father has bartered and traded, say, a barrel of apples for a fine fat goose, rather than take Continental money."

"Exactly!" continued Anselm. "These officers and soldiers, mostly Massachusetts men or at least New Englanders, formed a group called The Ohio Company of Associates and bartered with Congress to exchange the pay due them for land here in the Northwest."

Winthrop, who enjoyed driving a good bargain himself once in a while, asked shrewdly, "How much land?"

"Each share of stock costs one thousand dollars in Continental scrip plus ten dollars in hard cash. It entitles the holder to one lot at Campus Martius, a three-acre lot in town, and an eight-acre tract in the country. All are to be drawn by lottery so there will be no favoring of one shareholder over another. Care to join us?" Anselm asked, glancing sidewise at Winthrop.

"I — I want to go directly to General Putnam," he stated simply, without replying. Then he realized the demand might sound impertinent. "Would the General be too busy to see me now?"

"The General is busy, but he is not a man to turn anyone away," Anselm answered gravely. "He should be in his marquee on the Commons this time of morning. You'll see what a fine big tent it is, allotted to him at the division of the goods taken from General Burgoyne's army when the British surrendered at Saratoga. He little thought then what use he'd be putting it to. It's office, bedroom, and living quarters until his blockhouse in Campus Martius is completed."

As he led the way, Anselm chatted amiably. "Thanks chiefly to an organization of Revolutionary officers that call themselves The Order of the Cincinnati—after the famous

28

Roman soldier who left his plow still standing in the field when he went to obey a summons to fight for his fatherland —we've covered the landscape with Latin names. This, now, is Tiber Creek."

They all stepped aside to allow a yoke of oxen to pass over the high plank bridge.

"If the springs on the hillside prove true to their present promise, we'll build an aqueduct, just like the Romans. And there are large mounds up yonder—" He motioned north-eastward. "Someone heaped them up, many years ago. The savages disclaim any knowledge of them. Since we don't understand them, either, we have labeled them with names to puzzle the rest of the populace: Quadranaou, Capitolium, Conus, Sacra Via."

Suzanne frowned with concentration.

Anselm laughed. "There are those of us who find it pleasant." He began to sing, off-key:

Arise, my true love, and present me your hand,
*   And we'll march in procession for a far distant land*
Where the girls will card and spin
*   And the boys will plow and sow,*
And we'll settle on the banks of the pleasant O-hi-o!

Winthrop, absorbed in finding General Putnam and inquiring about his father, paid little heed to Anselm or to the surroundings. Still, he could hardly help noticing the strange cornfield through which their path led. None of the soil had been turned to the plow. The pale cornstalks stood where they had been planted by hoe, among stumps. Huge trees, still unfelled, were stripped of a broad band of bark; thus girdled, they would soon shed their leaves and sunlight would sift through their branches. With a miller's eye, he estimated that the yield from that planting of corn could be twenty bushels an acre, barring an early frost.

"Communal field," Anselm commented. "We'll culti-vate it when the carpenters and joiners have a little free time from their building activities."

They entered the shade of high-arching elms through which they could see a large Commons cleared, skirting the bank of the Muskingum for some distance. As they stepped into the sunlight, they threaded their way past a frenzy of activity—men, horses, and oxen heaving and pulling at freshly cut tree limbs, while other workmen were shaping, weaving, interlacing lighter branches for the overhead shel-tering "roof" of the crude structure.

"They're building a bowery—or, rather, rebuilding the one we had for our big Fourth of July banquet and celebra-tion. A heavy windstorm didn't help that any; besides, the leaves had grown brown and shriveled, needing replacing. This one is for the reception of His Excellency, General Arthur St. Clair, Governor of the Northwest Territory. He was escorted from Pittsburgh by a detachment of Fort Harmar troops about a week ago. He'll cross over from the fort on the government barge this afternoon, officially take the oath of office this 15th day of July, 1788, and do his first speech-making to the citizens here. You have landed just in time to help us celebrate."

Winthrop thought vaguely that Anselm had a touch of the schoolmaster about him. He looked ahead to the large tent his escort was pointing out to him. The flaps were turned back, opening it to the soft breeze.

General Rufus Putnam sat on a campstool at the plank table

As they drew near the marquee, Anselm asked soberly, in low voice, "What was it? River pirates, or Indians?"

"Indians."

"Near?"

"A night and a morning's journey upstream." Winthrop told him the story briefly.

"Major Tupper to see General Putnam. Urgent!"

General Rufus Putnam sat on a campstool at the plank table, where a pile of papers awaited his attention. Among them were a map of the ranges to be surveyed, a report estimating the strength of the Indian Nations, laborers' wage lists to be approved, plans for Campus Martius and its gardens, but most plaguing of all, the news brought by an express messenger two days before from the Falls of the Muskingum.

For several weeks, plans had been going forward for holding a treaty with the Indians at that spot of the Nations' own choosing, some sixty miles upriver. Soldiers had transported blankets, trinkets, gunpowder—all the usual "treaty goods"—by the canoe load. Then suddenly, before they had so much as finished unpacking their bales and displaying their offerings, and before they had got down to the slow business of treaty talk, they were attacked. Four of the soldiers from Fort Harmar were killed. Now a command was on its way to reinforce the ill-fated peace party, to bring back what was left of the supplies, to demand six Indians as hostages, and to inform the chiefs—who insisted the attack was made by a wandering band of Shawnees—that if there was to be a treaty, it must be held at Fort Harmar.

Putnam looked up and sighed, then folded his hands over the bulge of his waistcoat and regarded Anselm. "I see you have kept the polish on your military manners." He puckered his heavy-jowled face agreeably. "It would do no harm to apply a bit to your person and to wear your uniform occasionally."

"I have just returned from the plot being surveyed below the Seven Ranges, sir."

Putnam's head settled deeper into his shoulders. "What's this about urgent news?"

Anselm repeated the story Winthrop had told him.

Putnam winced from a twinge of pain from an old wound in his knee. "This bears out the warning from Pittsburgh. The tribes are restless. We must alert the laborers

32

again and dispatch a reconnoitering party to scout the forest nearby. You, Tupper, hire a hunter or a pilot who knows the Virginia shore; take an expedition up the Ohio and see if you can find trace of the lad's father." He thrust out his pendulous lower lip and muttered, "Still they curse me for ordering military duty for every able-bodied man!"

Putnam stared reflectively across the river toward Fort Harmar, for the moment forgetting Anselm's presence. The sad news of the soldiers killed at the Falls of the Muskingum was still heavy upon him. One of them, he recalled, was a Sergeant McKnight who had brought his wife to live outside the barracks. Mrs. McKnight had done chores and laundry and mending for the soldiers, and had sometimes been a target for their rough sense of humor. A final indignity had come while her husband was at the Falls with the expedition. A loutish private had given her a ducking in her own washtub while other soldiers stood by roaring with laughter. When word of her husband's death during the Indian attack at the Falls reached her, she had taken a skiff and rowed over to Putnam's marquee to beg refuge of him.

Putnam had given Mrs. McKnight temporary quarters in the partially built Campus Martius Stockade; here she had fetched her few belongings and was already setting up housekeeping. Of course! The Widow McKnight might be the answer to this immediate problem of what to do with the offspring of the lost man, Josiah Lake!

"Bring the young man in," General Putnam ordered.

Winthrop was prepared for a forbidding personage resplendent in the blue, buff, and gold-braided uniform of a general. He saw, instead, a stout, heavy-framed man in

33

sober black breeches and gray waistcoat, whose unpowdered hair was drawn back severely and tied with black tape.

"Winthrop Lake?" Putnam rumbled.

Winthrop noted that the prominent eyes under the bristling brows were kind. He found his voice. "Yes, sir."

The General brushed aside further preamble. "A party is being organized at once to search for your father. A miller, he is?"

"Yes, sir."

"I was bound over as apprentice to a miller when I was scarcely your age. What do you know of the business?"

"Only what I learned from helping around the mill."

"We shall have need of a miller here."

Winthrop's head came up higher, and there was unspoken fear in his eyes. Did the General think his father would not return?

Putnam saw the question. "Until the searching party locates your father or he makes it alone to Campus Martius —a tedious business in the wilderness—I believe the Widow McKnight may be persuaded to care for you and your sisters at Campus Martius. Except for Mrs. Owen, who is busy caring for the ailing General Varnum down at the Point, there are no women in the settlement as yet," he explained. Then he asked, "Will that be satisfactory?"

"Oh, thank you, sir!" Winthrop spoke his heartfelt gratitude. "For my sisters, that will be most kind of you. For myself, I must stay on the boat that brought us."

He blushed under Putnam's questioning glance. "The cargo is grist from our mill. From all accounts, river pirates passing in the night might hold it precious as gold."

"True, lad, and it is even more precious than gold to others." The General recalled the pale cornstalks in their communal field. "It will be better if you bring your boat up the Muskingum and tie up at the Campus Martius landing, instead. There it may be more closely guarded." Then he inquired briskly, "What do you propose to do in the daytime?"

"Anything you say, sir. I hope it may not be many days before—"

"The company is still surveying the lots in the bottom-lands and first river terrace of the Ohio and Muskingum. I assign you as camp boy and general helper. You will find it interesting and helpful."

Winthrop nodded, unable to speak.

"The pay is small. Seven dollars per month and two rations per day. The rations consist of a pound of pork or beef, venison or other wild meat equivalent, and vegetables whenever procured. You shall provide yourself with firearms and be subject to military law." As methodically as if he were adjusting a spyglass, General Putnam resumed the scrutiny of the papers at hand. "Major Tupper will escort you to Campus Martius."

Out on the newly cleared path once more, Suzanne moved timidly, keeping close to her brother's side. Merry was again delightedly riding atop Major Tupper's shoulder. The way led up a gentle slope past the sawpits, where whining of the saws and the regular thud of the workmen's mallets nearby gave promise of sawed planks and hewn timbers.

Winthrop suddenly stopped and stared in astonish-

"Campus Martius! It's larger than Fort Harmar!"

36

ment, pointing. "Campus Martius!" he cried. "It's even larger than Fort Harmar!"

"And when finished there will be no finer dwellings west of the Allegheny Mountains," said Anselm proudly.

The dwellings formed a hollow square. Anselm pointed to the four blockhouses, one rising at each corner. "The southeast one we're nearing, fronting on the Muskingum, will house General St. Clair. To the southwest, where the workmen are hammering away, is the communal hall to be used for meetings, courts of law, and the like. The northeast blockhouse will shelter the families as they arrive. Each man will be obliged to complete his outside wall and his share of the stockade itself within thirty days or he forfeits his right to build."

"Caution before comfort," Winthrop remarked briefly, finding Anselm's chatter instructive, but tiresome.

With one arm, Anselm graciously waved Suzanne toward the tall stockade's open gateway; with the other, he took the clinging Merry from his shoulder and set her on her feet. "Enter!" He swept them a low bow.

As they crossed the square studded with smoldering tree stumps, a woman with a large iron kettle and stick in hand was coming out of a doorway on the east side. Her skirt was pinned back and her starched cap and apron were unhampered by frills.

Winthrop surmised, from the way she went about the task of poking an ashen stump into a lively blaze, that her character, too, was free of frippery.

She looked up inquiringly when Anselm, leading the way across the square, called her name. With the back of her hand she rubbed hastily at the trace of tears on her smoke-smudged face. Her brown eyes warmed with pleasure as she saw Merry in Anselm's grip and Suzanne shyly following Winthrop.

"La!" she cried gaily, "females of my own kind! Which house here will you be neighboring in?"

"We are just stopping over, Kentucky-bound," Winthrop began; then he wished he had not spoken when he saw the shadow come over her face.

"This is the Lake family," Anselm told Mrs. McKnight. "The young Master Winthrop has just come from a visit with General Putnam," he added with a significant lift of his eyebrows.

Mrs. McKnight caught his signal of disaster. "Bless my soul!" Her lean cheeks pinked with agitation. She set aside the water-filled kettle and reached for Merry. "Bright as a new copper." She smiled at the child. "And hungry, too?"

"Yes." Merry slipped from Anselm's hold to go to her side. "I like maple sugar."

Mrs. McKnight turned to Suzanne and spoke as one woman to another. "Together we can cook a fitting breakfast. First, I'll set my kettle to boil. While wood is being burned, to clear the ground of stumps, why let its heat escape into thin air? Anyway, there are no chimneys as yet in any of the dwellings." She looked up at Anselm and directed, "You and Master Lake go to the river and wash up. I'll tend to the children."

When Winthrop looked back from the gateway, Mrs. McKnight was herding Merry and Suzanne into the doorway from which she had come.

CHAPTER THREE

Suzanne went quietly about her household chores in the kitchen, or keeping-room, of Mrs. McKnight's quarters facing the inner courtyard of Campus Martius. From the small bedroom adjoining, the widow sat at her mending, keeping a watchful eye on Merry.

It was late September. More than two months had passed since the Lakes had arrived. Much had happened in the little settlement, now officially named Marietta, in honor of the beautiful Queen Marie Antoinette of France and in recognition of her help to the American colonies during the Revolutionary War. With General—now Governor—Arthur St. Clair making this place his headquarters, Marietta was the capital of the whole great Territory Northwest of the River Ohio, extending westward to the Mississippi and northward to the Great Lakes.

In mid-August the first boatloads of families from New England had arrived and had been warmly welcomed. In early September the first Court in the Northwest Territory had been opened with great ceremony and a procession that led from the Point to Campus Martius. Since there were no cases to be tried, it adjourned promptly.

With so much going on here, Suzanne thought, reasonably, there could also be many things that might detain her father. If he had been injured, a passing boatman might have

39

taken him aboard and tended his wounds. He might even now be making his way toward Campus Martius from far down the river. Or a trapper might be nursing him to health in some remote hut. She refused to believe that he had been killed. Though the searching party had returned with no news of her father, Suzanne was sure that one day when the need for him became strongest, he would come.

As a child, when things were fretting her, she had sometimes turned to a secret charm for help. Maybe today, although she was old enough now, of course, to question it, the charm might work, might give her some promise of her father's return.

Impulsively, she set aside the turkey-feather duster and went to the window. She closed her eyes, waited until her mind was clear of everything but expectancy, then opened them quickly. What she saw was a patch of deep-blue sky marked out in a long V, a flock of wild geese winging southward in high, clean precision. Her heart lurched with delight. It was a sign! Yes, the honking geese were calling her to hasten outside.

There was only the broad kitchen hearth to be tidied before her chores for the day would be done. The two ground-floor rooms that had been assigned to Mrs. McKnight were seldom in disarray, but even so the sparse furnishings must be moved and dusted. "It is our duty to be industrious," the never-idle housewife liked to say. Suzanne sighed, thinking of the hours she had spent patching clothes that did not quite need it, scrubbing corners that were already spotless, and storing away things "for the hard days to come." The hard days gave no real threat of coming, but Widow McKnight shook her head and clucked her tongue, "Take my word for it and be grateful you have not yet experienced a winter in the wilderness—as I have." And she would recount the long months when Fort Harmar had been on half rations, or less.

After scrubbing the hearthstone, Suzanne went to the bedroom. The bright afternoon light fell upon Mrs. McKnight's starched housecap and the gathered folds of her skirt. A scarf of bleached linen was crossed over her bosom. Mrs. McKnight was quite proper about her attire now that more families were arriving and one might expect callers. She looked up now with a smile.

"A young man at the Point speared a large pike last night and will share it for the asking. It would be wrong for the lad's fish to go begging. Would you oblige me by fetching us a bit for our supper?"

"Oh, yes!" Suzanne answered eagerly.

"Me too, Susu! Take me!" Merry clamored, suddenly appearing from under the counterpane where she had been quietly engaged in some game of her own.

"Land sakes! Merry Lake!" Mrs. McKnight chided. "When will you learn that respectable children speak softly and walk, instead of running?"

Suzanne, bending to tie Merry's shawl under her chin, failed to notice the indulgent smile that deepened the creases about Mrs. McKnight's eyes. "She's not quite four," Suzanne reminded her. Straightening, she blushed. "I meant no disrespect, ma'am."

"Of course not, my child!" the woman said brusquely. "You are right to take up for her, things being as they are.

41

There, now, I've snarled a thread. Mind you're back before dusk." Her gaze followed Suzanne and Merry to the door and lingered there awhile after they had gone.

The morning had been cool and dew had dripped like rain from the trees. Now, as Suzanne led Merry along the road to the Point, the sun came warmly through the trees. In the clearings, goldenrod dimmed, the grass was tall and brittle, and the tips had formed tiny heads.

From Fort Harmar distant sounds of an Indian chant blew across the river and through the forest.

"What are they singing?" Merry asked.

"I don't know," Suzanne answered. "Maybe they are trying to tell us they were the first to have homes along these rivers."

"It's scary."

"They're just people." Suzanne tried to reassure herself as well as Merry. "We must greet them as brothers. Governor St. Clair has ordered it."

Merry was satisfied, though she did not understand. "Here come some of them across the river!" She pointed to three long graceful canoes speeding toward the Point.

Suzanne stopped and leaned against a large oak at the outskirts of the huts that formed the settlement there. Her heart was thudding heavily. Her first thought was to turn back toward Campus Martius, but how could she fail to carry out Mrs. McKnight's simple request to obtain a bit of fish for their supper? She would, indeed, be thought a weakling to run at sight of a few harmless Indians. They were restless as a flock of birds, never stopping long in one place. Likely as not they would put on some brief ceremony now, as was their custom, and then be gone. "Maybe they will sing and dance, Merry. That would be fun to watch, wouldn't it?"

Merry jumped up and down with excitement. "Let's!"

Suzanne noticed uneasily that women and children at the Point were running into their cabins, in spite of the Governor's orders to be hospitable. She heard the bolting of doors. As the Indians swarmed over the bank, she hastily boosted Merry into the branches of the tree and climbed after her. By bending back a leafy bough they could look into the Commons where the warriors were assembling around the flagpole; yet they would not be seen.

The warriors were smeared all over with ceremonial color: some red, some black, some decorated with painted insects or with bold zigzags. It had the effect of marking out all their features except their eyes, which alone seemed alive.

A drum beat flatly and a high thin voice began a wailing song. Slowly it was caught up by other voices and mingled with the scuffing of feet in rhythm with the drum. The tone quickened, deepened. A wild chant rose and the dancers sprang into a circle around the flagpole.

Suddenly Suzanne was aware of footsteps coming softly through the brush at the rim of the clearing. An Indian appeared and leaned against the mottled gray-brown trunk of a nearby sycamore. He wore undressed deerskin leggings and white moccasins decorated with silver ornaments that shone against the leaf-strewn ground. There were two eagle feathers braided in his glistening hair. As he slowly turned his face toward the dancers, his expression dream-filled and sad, Suzanne felt a stab of recognition. It was the Indian they had seen that night in the flash of lightning on the river!

The branch under her hand snapped. The Indian looked up sharply. His eyes were blue! Suzanne drew back into the foliage and froze with terror against the tree trunk.

Merry, attracted by the gleaming moccasins, parted the leaves and smiled through. "Pretty shoes!"

"Hush!" Suzanne whispered and drew her close. At least, she managed to reason above her rising panic, he made no move to come toward them. He stood staring up, first at Suzanne, with blue eyes fathomless as an iced-over pond; then at Merry, with a gaze that seemed to light with a glimmer of pleasure. He looked at his silver-trimmed moccasins, then back again at Merry and, before he moved swiftly into the underbrush, he turned and gazed at her over his shoulder.

"Where'd he go?" Merry blinked her amber eyes in disbelief at the Indian's sudden disappearance.

"I don't know." Suzanne slid from the tree and lifted Merry to the ground. "Let's leave before he comes back."

"I don't want to!" Merry began to whimper.

Without a word, Suzanne gathered the little girl in her arms and began running along the deep-rutted road leading toward Campus Martius. Once she thought she heard the soft pad of moccasined feet following, but peering fearfully into the forest behind her, she saw no one. The plaintive beat of the Indians' music grew fainter. She slowed to a trot as she passed the communal field, and forced herself to a walk when she came within sound of the saws snarling at the pit where workmen were using the last daylight.

Safe in Widow McKnight's kitchen, she untied Merry's

hood and leaned exhausted and a little out of breath against the window frame.

Mrs. McKnight came in briskly, and stopped abruptly. "Suzanne, child, are you ailing?"

"No, Mrs. McKnight."

"But you do look peaked." She went to the cupboard and took out a bottle. "Oil of juniper, child. This will cure you of anything." She proffered the spoon.

Suzanne obediently swallowed the bitter tonic. "I didn't get the fish. I should have stayed," she murmured.

"We can do very well without it."

"There were Indians—" Suzanne began.

"Nonsense! You must grow accustomed to the savages coming in and being around," Mrs. McKnight interrupted sternly, "especially now, when they're trying to assemble delegates from all the tribes that feel they have claim to this Northwest Territory. Word is around that we're to expect Cornplanter, Chief of the Senecas, with about forty of his tribesmen, ready to take part in the peace treaty. They will be escorted, mind you, by troops from Fort Pitt on this peace mission. The Cornplanter is a great and friendly chief. Even so low-ranking a soldier as Sergeant McKnight knew that. Suzanne, you have nothing to fear from the Cornplanter or his warriors."

"Was it Cornplanter who caught us hiding in the tree?" Merry asked. She tossed her curls. "I wasn't afraid of him. He wore pretty shoes, all shiny."

Widow McKnight patted Merry in an absentminded manner and reached into a crock for a maple sugar lump to quiet the child.

"There was one special Indian, alone," Suzanne insisted, uncertain how to explain.

The woman turned away. "The candles are ready to take out of the mold and trim," she directed. "How grateful we should be to General Putnam for giving us the tallow!" Work was one great cure-all for one's troubles, she felt. One could forget them if one had enough—or even too much—work to do. Indians? Pshaw! During all her days of following Sergeant McKnight to this and that outpost, they had been the least of her fears. She did not understand Suzanne's fancies. The girl had been raised for a gentler life than she herself had known.

It was late by the time Suzanne had finished with the candles and the supper work was done. It was growing colder, too, so that Suzanne pulled the covers closer around Merry before she gently lifted the music box from her tiny hands, loosened with sleep. From overhead came the muffled sounds of roistering as newcomers, a roomful of adventure-seeking young men from New England, celebrated their arrival at last in "Putnam's Paradise." In the kitchen, Mrs. McKnight registered her disapproval by vigorously poking at her ceiling with the broomstick. There was other noise, too. From beyond the thin walls separating their quarters from those of a well-behaved family recently arrived from Vermont, came the wail of a baby, youngest of the seven children and evidently not yet completely schooled in how to behave. From somewhere, too, came the sound of pounding. The dwellings at Campus Martius were being completed and being occupied. Still Merry slept. Suzanne smiled down at her. Then she went to the window.

Mrs. McKnight poked vigorously at her ceiling

There was no candle gleaming from the window of the little Land Office building. Nor was there a flicker of torch-light down by their boat. Winthrop, then, had not yet re-turned from the surveying tract. She longed to tell him of her encounter this afternoon, though by now she was angry with herself and a little ashamed—and consequently disliked the Indian who made her feel that way! She should not have been frightened, should not have run away like a silly child. After all, this Indian with the "pretty shoes," might pos-sibly have had word of her father. The feeling she had had, that the long wedge of winging geese was some kind of omen, might not have been so fanciful, after all. And she had run away!

CHAPTER FOUR

The morning sky was still hung with stars when Winthrop and Anselm launched their dugout canoe off a shoal some fifty-five miles upstream on the Muskingum. The river was at low stage after the dry summer months. For a while it took all Winthrop's attention at the bow paddle to follow the larger canoe ahead where John Matthews, surveyor, and Sam Patchen, his new assistant from the District of Maine, were leading the way along the dark channels toward the Falls of the Muskingum. Finally, as daylight brimmed over the hills and lifted the fog, Winthrop had only to match Anselm's strokes. Once more the search for his father rose uppermost in his mind.

Anselm sensed his mood. "Let me remind you, Winthrop, that our searching party found three dead Indians at that creek mouth and no sign of any more. It stands to reason that your father got away."

Winthrop gazed over the river valley that was tinged with autumn. "Almost three months have passed."

They went on a while in silence, keeping in the wake of the dugout in which Corporal Van Berckle and Private Mason, guards from Fort Harmar, rode, muskets on knees.

"General Putnam must have a few qualms for our safety," Winthrop ventured. "This is the first time he's ordered out a guard to travel with us."

" 'Twas not General Putnam's doing. The guard was ordered by Governor St. Clair. He's got his dander up since the plans for a parley at the Falls went awry and since some of the tribes are so slow about coming in to treat at Fort Harmar. Yonder is yet another reason—" Anselm tipped his paddle toward the bank where a skinned deer carcass rotted in the sun. "The more warlike tribes are resentful of having their 'beloved bear grounds,' as they call this whole area, intruded upon. They're killing off game as close to the settlement as possible, often just leaving it to decay. Our hunters brought intelligence only yesterday that there's hardly a deer, bear, or turkey to be found within a radius of twenty miles around Campus Martius."

"It seems odd," Winthrop said moodily, "that you New Englanders would leave your settled farms and villages for this."

"After the war most of us had little choice." Anselm shrugged. "And a fair land it is, or will be as soon as we have it tamed a bit."

Winthrop grinned over his shoulder at him, wrinkling his nose in the direction of the rotting deer carcass.

"Look beyond your nose and this is a remarkable settle-ment," the other insisted. "In the history of mankind, no such experiment in planned colonization has ever been made."

"Oh, sure, it's full of ideas," Winthrop agreed absently. "Schooling and worshiping provided for, a system of courts —"

"There's more than that!" Anselm drove his paddle deep for emphasis. "Men who fought for independence and took

49

this land as their pay wanted a good way of life; they would not take any part of this country until they were assured of their way. They saw to it that an ordinance was drawn up for the governing of this Northwest Territory and they dropped in one provision that was like throwing a billet of wood into a hornets' nest."

"What was it?" Winthrop was mildly interested.

"That this colony will not remain a colony. In time we will become a state, on equal footing with any of the states, big or little, old or new. Such a far-sighted plan is having its beginning here," Anselm concluded.

At midday the canoes grounded on a willow-fringed sandbar. Winthrop stood up, stretched, climbed over the gear of blankets, firearms, and surveying equipment and un-packed the few necessary utensils and provisions for meal-getting. Anselm joined John Matthews on a beached log to pore over the map of the range to be surveyed. They were old hands at this, Winthrop knew. A year before the Ohio Company had made its purchase, they had been with a party under Thomas Hutchins, Chief Geographer of the United States, to survey the Seven Ranges laid out along the Ohio directly north of the Company's acres.

Winthrop made a small hollow in the sand for his fire; then he went into the underbrush to gather an armful of dry branches. Returning, he paused to look over John Matthew's shoulder. The map was neat and finely drawn. "Our findings must accurately compare with these drawings of Hutchins's, as to observations on the needle and meridian," Matthews was explaining to Sam Patchen.

"Oh, my soul, Corporal Van Berckle!" muttered Private

Mason, who was lounging nearby in the shade of the corporal's broad back. "My innards scream for victuals, while yonder camp boy stands gaping at a map!"

Winthrop turned, scowling. Corporal Van Berckle was a campaign-battered fellow with a thatch of yellow hair. One would know him to be Pennsylvania Dutch even before he spoke. The lanky Private Mason, on the other hand, had the appearance of a hard-sinewed Vermonter. Winthrop's scowl vanished as he saw the look of raillery on their goodnatured, weathered faces. "You'll sing for your meal yet," he quipped, and sauntered off with great deliberateness to build his fire.

The soldiers promptly took Winthrop's remark literally. They leaned their heads together and sang:

> The Duke's a bold commander; the Duke's a bold
>   commander;
> He leads his forces to the field as bold as Alexander.
> He'll die before he'll yield.
> He'll die before he'll run.
> Sound every trumpet, sound, boys!
> Let every man stand his ground, boys!
> He'll never flinch, nor start back an inch,
> So let his health go round, boys.

Soon the meal was ready, and soon the last morsel of pork was spooned from the thick stew. John Matthews sighed with satisfaction, before rising to announce the plans for the afternoon's activities.

"Anselm, you know this section of the tract, so it may be best for you to lead on with the guard," he suggested. "Our camp boy has earned a rest. Patchen and I will take him with us in the dugout with the gear."

51

They glided through the clear channels, the warm fall sun golden on the willows at the water's edge. Winthrop, settled among the bundles, let his thoughts travel ahead. It was useless to plan his search, he realized. The wilderness was a vast and secret place. But today, at least, he determined not to be hampered by the slow pace of the surveyors. He would scout for the most likely route a lost man might have taken, and follow it, alone, on the pretense of hunting meat for camp.

He fastened his gaze on the smooth-muscled swing of John Matthews's arms. Paddling came naturally to him. With Sam Patchen, it was different. Sam's lean shoulders were stooped, and his near-sighted squint suggested that he was more accustomed to sitting on a stool at a desk than in the stern of a dugout canoe.

"I couldn't stay there any longer," Patchen was saying, "and live upon air that had passed through half a dozen sets of lungs before it came to mine. Now, this is to my liking!" Their craft veered a little as Sam's paddle swept a wide arc in the air to include all the nearby landscape.

"Then look well this afternoon," Matthews told him. "We'll be surveying a portion of the Donation Lands, one hundred acres for each, to be drawn by lottery."

Patchen missed another stroke. "What would the lucky winners be bound to do?"

"Well, that has not been decided," Matthews answered thoughtfully, "but we'll be hearing more of it. The main purpose is to form small groups that will serve as outposts to the Ohio Company's Purchase."

Patchen coughed. "What could one lose?"

Matthews turned toward him, grinning wryly. "His scalp," he said.

"Mine's balding already," Patchen remarked. "I'd not mind chancing it. I'd be cheating the poor savages."

The Falls of the Muskingum, when they reached them, proved to be nothing more than some rapids shrunken by the dry summer to a thin trickle over mossy ledges. Matthews beached on the rocky east bank. Winthrop leaped into the shallows, pulled the dugout by its prow onto a sand spit nearby, and began to unload the surveying equipment.

Anselm bent with the private and the corporal over what appeared to be deer tracks in the mud, motioning absently to Winthrop to leave the gear stowed. "We'll look around before we proceed to the range."

Corporal Van Berckle shouldered his musket and started up the faint trail leading into the underbrush. "Ach! Deer tracks, is it? I say it gives the tracks of an unshod pony!"

Private Mason rolled his watery eyes and polished a bullet against his sleeve. "Fresh sign or no, something sets my old campaign wound to itching!"

Signs there were, Winthrop noticed, as he followed the men up the trail, that this place was a favorite locality for both men and animals. Still, the forest was creeping jealously close to cover the marks made by the last large encampment near the Falls. A second growth was pushing up from the tree roots in the clearing that the garrison soldiers had made for the ill-fated parley last summer. The huts and shelters for provisions and ammunition were now heaps of vine-clad logs. The half-finished Council House sagged, loose strips of bark flapping in the breeze.

Corporal Van Berckle used his boot-toe to stir the sodden coals in the hollow of the ground. "It appears no fire has been lit here since my comrades, Sergeant McKnight and the others, were killed."

Private Mason, still suspiciously skirting the clearing, pointed to a broken bow half covered with sand. "Delaware," he pronounced, and bent to examine the bow more closely. "Faith! The paint on it is still fresh!"

Anselm looked inquiringly at Matthews and Patchen. "What do you say now to our surveying?"

"I say we'd better get to it while the sun is still high," Matthews answered firmly.

"Yes, yes!" Patchen agreed impatiently.

"Then we'll start the north ridge," Anselm decided.

While Winthrop unpacked the surveying equipment, he took his bearings and saw a small stream emptying above the falls. A man, lost, would most likely follow a stream, not only for water but also as a way to eventually reach a river, the most traveled highway of the wilderness. Winthrop decided to cut overland from the council site and explore along the creek's course on foot.

He returned to the clearing and unloaded tally pins, standard chain, field books, theodolite, compass, mapping paper, and goose quills sharpened to varying degrees of pointedness for pen-work.

Private Mason shook his head comically. " 'Pon my word! Those are innocent looking implements with which to invade a wilderness such as this!"

Laughingly, the surveyors took up their equipment. At the edge of the clearing Anselm looked back. "Step lively,

Winthrop. We're keeping close together on this jaunt."

But Winthrop swung his musket to the crook of his arm.

"I'm going up-creek—for game."

Anselm hesitated, understanding the lad's true purpose. It was at odds with his own better judgment, but seeing the determination in Winthrop's face, he nodded him on. "But take care," he cautioned. "Mark your trail well. We'll meet here by sundown."

Winthrop pushed on alone into the silent woods. He set himself an easy pace through three furlongs of timber freed of underbrush by Indian hunting fires, loped down a hillside bright overhead with persimmon and festoons of bittersweet, then broke through waist-high cane and into a briar thicket edging the creek. With his eye he measured the distance of the leap across. Next moment, foot poised in the air, he paused.

Something was splashing along the creek bed, just out of sight, behind an overhanging rock about a rod upstream. He drew quickly back into the brush; he tried to fight down the hope and dread that were making his flesh quiver. His eyes bored through the thicket to the water eddying under the rock. As the sound came closer, his finger inched along the smooth musket stock toward the trigger. A furry snout, two immense paws, and then the heavy body of a large she-bear appeared from around the rock. Just then the wind must have changed, or perhaps Winthrop let out his with-held breath, for abruptly, at no movement from himself of which he was aware, the bear stopped, reared to its hind legs, and stood sniffing the air for the direction in which

The bear reared to its hind legs and sniffed the air

danger lay. Suddenly she snorted, dropped to all fours, and
splashed across the creek into the thorny thicket.

Winthrop leaped the creek and beat his way into the
brambles with his musket butt. The bear crashed from the
brush and broke for timber. Winthrop, marking the place
where it disappeared into a beech grove, fell flat over a
hidden ditch. He picked himself up, crouched low, and
began a methodical stalking of his quarry. Meat for the
hungry settlement! He mustn't let it escape him. Just as he
was bending lower to make his way under the branches of
pine, a slanting ray of sun glinted on a sizeable patch of
brown fur. He raised his loaded musket, fired—and missed!
The bear bounded in a frenzy of rage and terror through a

bed of may apples and scrambled for a foothold up a rocky crevasse. Clumps of fern came off in Winthrop's grasping hands as he clawed his way in pursuit.

Halfway to the top, he paused for breath and looked up to see the bear disappear over the ridge. With a final burst of effort, Winthrop scaled the precipice. From the distant side of a large meadow, the bear's hindquarters blended into the forest. Exhausted, Winthrop sank to the ground and gave up the chase. When his lungs no longer felt that they were bursting, he sat up to take his bearings. He looked about in wonder.

It was as if he had come upon another world. The vast saddle of meadowland rimmed by stately pines seemed so close to the clouds that he felt he could reach up and touch them. Beyond the sentinel pines, the wooded hills fell away on all sides into the autumn haze. Far to the south, the Muskingum shone in silver loops. Here summer lingered, with a golden touch upon the green turf and the thin crystal stream threading through it. Winthrop went to the stream and drank deeply.

There was something about the place that caught at his memory. He sat, chin on knees, and then he remembered. He visualized a time far back when, as a small child, he had left the house of his mother's people in the tidewater country of Maryland and had journeyed with his parents by ox-wagon toward a new home in Ligonier Valley. The mountain meadow where they stopped to rest one golden afternoon might have been this one. The stream shining at his feet was very like the one near which his mother had laid the clean quilt and sat beside him while his father unyoked the oxen. He remembered her voice now, full of sweetness, as she turned the handle of the music box and sang:

The seed is blown before the wind
And where it comes to rest
Be it on mountain meadow green—

"Nearly eleven years ago," he said half aloud, and the sound of his words startled him. Now his mother's voice with its endearing French accent was stilled—and who knew what had become of his father? Winthrop rose abruptly, checking his thoughts. He let his eyes rove once more over the smooth meadow before he turned to retrace his way.

The chase had led him farther than he realized. Already the sun was sinking behind the hills. What had the day brought? Nothing but an aching heart and empty hands. He lengthened his stride, pausing only once to pick up a hickory log for the supper fire. Tomorrow, he vowed, nothing should turn him from his search.

When Winthrop broke through the clearing, Anselm, sitting with his back against the dilapidated Council House, leaped to his feet. Corporal Van Berckle and Private Mason, standing guard by the river trail, slowly lowered their muskets. Matthews straightened from tightening the thongs about his blanket roll, and Patchen sighed in relief.

"Expecting someone else?" Winthrop forced a cheerful grin.

Anselm brushed aside Winthrop's question. "Thank heaven, you're safe! We're returning at once to Campus Martius."

"We are?" Winthrop dropped the log and looked from face to face. "But what of the surveying? I thought we'd be encamped for at least a week—" His voice trailed off. Another avenue of his search was closing.

John Matthews walked over to him and put a hand on his shoulder. "A scout came in with intelligence that there's a hostile band of Delawares nearby," he explained. "He also carried an order from General St. Clair for our return."

"It's a bitter thing to understand, lad." Anselm spoke consolingly. "But there must be no trouble that would endanger the plans for the treaty. The Indians don't like our surveying expeditions. They won't come to parley as long as we keep carving up the land."

The Vermonter rubbed his bony chin thoughtfully. "There's more kick in those instruments than I credited them with!"

As they slipped quietly downstream through the darkness, Winthrop's hand went to his hunting shirt pocket. For a long while he turned the powder horn cap in his hand. If Governor St. Clair suspended all surveying activities, how was he to continue his search?

CHAPTER FIVE

Josiah lay on a pile of furs in the corner of the pole hut. Through half-closed eyes he watched the coals snap and crackle in the middle of the dirt floor, and traced the wreath of smoke to the opening in the roof, a loosely meshed covering of bark and brush. Where the deerskin was drawn back from the door, the sunlight lay in an oblong of dusty gold. Outside, an Indian was drawing water from a creek.

Josiah had lain there, in weakness and fever, he knew not how long. But now he felt that he could sit up. With effort, he raised himself, pressing back the pain in his side. He moistened his lips and called the name he had learned.

"Silverheels!"

The Indian emerged from the flicker of sunlight and shadows under the trees. His preoccupied gaze quickened with interest as he noticed Josiah's improvement. Josiah stared back incredulously, his breath quickening. It had not been part of his delirium. The Indian's eyes were blue!

"*Shemanose weshelashamama yewaughsu,*" Silverheels murmured in a low monotone in the Shawanoese tongue.

Josiah's face showed his perplexity.

The Indian squatted on the floor, and spoke slowly and clearly in English. "The American is well. That is good."

Josiah lay back on the furs and wondered if this was still part of the fever.

"You surprised?" A ghost of a smile played across the thin lips. "*Notha English-manake*. My father an English-man. *Neegah Shawanoese*. My mother a Shawnee. Once I was message runner for our tribe." He glanced at his silver-trimmed moccasins. "Very fleet. When I run my feet flash in the sun." He stared pensively into the embers. "Now I run no more, and I dwell alone."

Josiah raised himself again and looked down at his side. Silverheels pushed him firmly back upon the skins.

"Do not touch," he said. Then, with a swift movement, he lifted and threw into the fire what appeared to be a poultice of slippery elm bark. Josiah, looking at the bared wound, saw that it had been neatly sutured. Silverheels reached into the otter-skin bag at his belt, measured a por-tion of powder into a hollowed stone bowl, and poured over it some water from a bark receptacle. With a smooth flint he laid the salve, pungent of pine and herbs, across the wound.

"You have taken care of me," Josiah spoke gratefully.

Silverheels allowed himself a small expression of pride. "My ancestors of the sacred Medewiwin cult. Have taught me many secrets for healing."

"How long have you cared for me?"

"The moon rises heavy. The corn stands in shocks, and the *pacan,* wild nuts, of the forest fall. Soon comes snow to cover *Ake,* earth, and ice to still the Muskingum and the Bald Eagle creek by Silverheels' lodge."

Relief ran through Josiah as he learned he was already at the Muskingum. But then the anxiety he had felt through his delirium returned. "I must go at once to Campus Mar-tius."

"Not yet strong enough. The journey is from sun to sun. Do not fear for your son and daughters."

"You know?"

Silverheels nodded. "White man talk much in sleep."

Josiah struggled to his feet. "I must find them at once." His legs shambled crazily. The walls of the hut began to slide and tilt through a dimming mist. He felt the breath knocked out of him and realized he had fallen to the floor.

Silverheels loosed Josiah's shirt and held something acrid under his nose, laid him again on the pile of furs, and tucked his bare feet under a blanket. He sat by, waiting for Josiah to regain his strength. Then he spoke. "While yet you drifted with the arrow in your side, I saw them. The girl and the child I saw again at the place they call Marietta, on the point where the Shawnee warriors danced."

At last Josiah was able to ask cautiously, "They were well? And the boy?"

Silverheels nodded silently.

During the pause in which he searched for a way to thank Silverheels, Josiah realized also that he must know a few facts. "Why did you bring me here?"

Silverheels shrugged, and his face looked as if he had pulled a curtain over it. "White man ask too much questions." He rose to leave the hut.

"Silverheels!" Josiah called in desperation. "I ask of you one final favor. Bring my children to me. I will pay!"

Silverheels turned on him a look of puzzled contempt and drew from beneath his belt a small purse of fine-dressed skin sewn with leather thongs. He let it drop to the floor as if it were offensive. "Has not been opened."

Josiah made no move to retrieve the purse. Some instinct warned him against protesting that it was not his.

"I mean no insult," he said, and met the Indian's gaze levelly. "I only want my children to know I am safe."

"Little man believe he safe with Silverheels?" The blue eyes glinted with a peculiar humor. "I go now to prepare Pimook."

Josiah's feverish eyes followed Silverheels as he heaped stones the size of large turnips upon an outdoor fire. Pimook? Had he offended Silverheels so that he was preparing some refined torture? When the stones were red-hot, Silverheels rolled them into a sort of oven of split plank and dirt built on the slope of the bank, one half within the earth, the other above ground. It looked, Josiah observed with a creeping horror, just the size in which to burn a man alive! Now the Indian threw something to boil in a large kettle swung over the fire. When he came back, he was carrying a small basin of the brew.

"Drink!" he commanded.

Josiah would have protested but, at the light of mockery in the blue eyes, he took the cup silently.

Once more Silverheels went outside. Josiah watched, weak with dread, as the Indian went to the creek, returned with a large gourd full of water, lifted the skin flap over the oven door, and threw the water inside on the hot stones. When steam began to rise, he closed the flap, came back to the hut, and stood towering over Josiah. "You walk now?"

Josiah lay still, unable to rise. A trickle of perspiration ran between his wide, dark eyes.

"Little man sweat too soon. Sweat with fear? Must not.

"Drink!" he commanded

Pimook good medicine. When Indian tired from travel, hunt, or war, he go into Pimook. Makes well. Brings rest, hunger, and strength. Come now." He placed a strong hand under Josiah's arm.

After Silverheels pulled him from the sweat oven onto waiting warm blankets and helped him again into the lodge, Josiah felt a delicious drowsiness run along his muscles, flexible now and free of aches. His eyes showed the gratitude he was too weary to speak.

Silverheels nodded in satisfaction. "I go now."

Josiah moistened his lips, but no words would come. He could only hope it was to Putnam's settlement that Silverheels was going.

For a few minutes after Silverheels had closed the deerskin over the door, Josiah lay still. Only his eyes roved around the hut. Yes, there on a peg in the corner hung his powder horn, his butternut-dyed homespun breeches, and his boots. On the floor the sewn purse still lay untouched.

He remembered now the scene on the river. He had reached the trapper too late to save him, but had pulled alongside to see if the man had anything that might identify him, anything to pass along to his kin. As he had bent to remove the packet from the trader's breeches, an arrow had bit deep into his side. But before consciousness welled out of him, Josiah had stuffed the wallet into his own pocket. His last memory was of lying in the bottom of the canoe, helplessly drifting. There, he supposed, Silverheels had found him. He reached sleepily for the purse now, and put it into his shirt. With a smile on his face at the hope of seeing his children soon, Josiah drifted into deep slumber.

For several hours after leaving Josiah, Silverheels sat on the western shore where the Bald Eagle spilled over the shallow rapids of the Muskingum. His lodge was not visible, though it was only a few rods back in the trees and heavy undergrowth. Silverheels had artfully concealed it against the predatory Delawares, whose canoe route lay this way, and against the prying eyes of meddlesome white soldiers. His heart was troubled with an old sorrow, and his thoughts again confused by the question of loyalties. It was a painful problem to him who had believed he had withdrawn into the life of an indifferent observer.

The gods of the forest were burning their crimson and gold fires in the ancient sacrament of September, but before them he could not warm his spirit. They withheld the solace and contentment he sought, silently rebuking him with the fact that for too long he had absented himself from their customs and rituals. Silverheels reminded himself that he was, after all, part white. But he was not a white man, he admitted bitterly.

The white man had let him go to their places of learning, their places of worship, their public buildings that were for all to enjoy. At the same time, they had set up a barrier by never looking into his eyes as man to man; their handshake fell away without the warm pressure of brotherly love; a smile on their lips did not welcome, but patronized him.

At first he had been angry, but the barrier was nothing he could combat with tomahawk or arrow, nor could he provoke an open insult which would justify his defending his honor in a contest of armed skill. He had begun to feel like the dappled fawns of the forest that white men tamed and then slaughtered when they were tired of playing with them.

And he had begun to look with a new detachment into the ways of the white people. In them he saw a cruelty that was not swift and clean and necessary, as among the so-called "savages." He watched the white leaders offering peace and friendship to the Indians while craftily drawing treaties that were designed to rob them of their very existence. Soon, even the houses of the settlers became offensive, unnatural structures imposed on the good earth against her will.

Sick in spirit, he had cast the white man's ways and his books and his clothes from him and returned to the woodland haunts of his young manhood, hungry for the simple, vigorous, and just mode of life of the Shawnees who had reared him.

How could he have forgotten the proud legend that the Shawnees were the first people created by the Master of Life, and that all other red men were descended from them? There were none superior, red or white, to these people. They had scorned the lazy life. Through a long period of wandering, hunting, and fighting all across the land from the place of their origin, far to the south along the Suwanee River, they had kept themselves strong and free from taint by inferior tribes. They were a small tribe, but a proud and fearless one. There were no weaklings. With his old fleetness, Silverheels had returned, running the maze of trails leading to their camps. They greeted him with eyes that were cold and suspicious. He was no longer invited to join the hunt, to come and go with the warriors, to dance at the ceremonials, or to sit at the feasts. Nor was he asked to run the ridge trails with messages. Loneliness settled with him in his lodges. And so he wandered, hovering about the fringe of the white settlements or about the outskirts of the Shawnee villages, leaving each hut, built lightly of logs, branches, and bark, to the desolation of the winds, when none brought peace.

This one he could leave without regret, except that in it he had something to care for. The little dark man was undoubtedly of the kind who had come to live at the Wa-ka-ta-me-sepe, the town on the river side, at the Eagle River which they called the Ohio. These people had been kind, without insult, except for the soldiers at Fort Harmar. These settlers from the country along the far ocean did not have the fierceness and treachery of the Virginia Long-knives. They lived in brotherly peace and shared their crops in the manner of Indians.

He still could not bring himself to go to the Kitchok-ema, the great chief St. Clair who had now arrived to rule the territory and who was notoriously out of sympathy with the Indians. Nor would he seek out the Shemagana, the soldier at Fort Harmar. Nor could he bear to set foot in the garrison on the plain of the Muskingum, erected so rudely over the graves of his ancestors. But to the children of the small brave man he had tended, he might go.

Silverheels rose, a small measure of joy and anticipation lifting his sense of loneliness. Once more he would carry a message! For a little while again he was honored; he was called upon to do a service he could perform well.

CHAPTER SIX

On the afternoon following his return from the Falls of the Muskingum, Winthrop sat with Suzanne on the crown of the cone-shaped mound southeast of Campus Martius. He looked thoughtfully down over the treetops to the newly erected pickets backing the Point, as he listened to her tale of the Indian she and Merry had encountered.

"You're sure he was the one we saw that night in the storm?" he asked.

"Yes," Suzanne insisted.

Merry, playing nearby with a small hoard of nuts in her willow basket, came closer to listen. "Indian looked sad," she offered.

Winthrop reached over and rumpled Merry's copper curls. "Be a good girl and go about your nutting. Mrs. McKnight is expecting enough to store for the winter." He turned again to Suzanne. "Like as not we'll never see him again."

"That's just the trouble," Suzanne murmured in self-reproach. "If only I hadn't been afraid. I have a feeling he could have told us something about Father."

"Females and their feelings!" Winthrop scoffed good-naturedly. "What we need is action."

It was then that Merry saw Silverheels. "Indian's come back!" she cried in delight, and pointed to him, looking up at them from the dry moat ringing the base of the mound. He was wearing the same undressed deerskin leggings and silver-trimmed moccasins, but now a quiver of arrows hung from one wide shoulder, and his glittering eyes were watchful. Merry impulsively snatched a handful of scarlet maple leaves and ran down the slope to meet him.

"Merry! Merry!" shouted Suzanne. She sat trembling on the ground and her voice fell hoarsely to a whisper. "Winthrop, go after her. I—I can't. It *is* the one, the one I saw looking up like that—" She would have said more, but Winthrop rose without listening. He wiped his dusty hands on his breeches, and walked slowly down the mound.

"The same face I saw in the lightning, too," he thought. "What does this Indian want? Why does he follow us? Why do his strange eyes look so at Merry?" A sudden panic of fear for the little girl's safety swept over him. He wished he had not left his musket, powder horn, and bullet pouch behind at the guardhouse. Against this tall, heavily muscled figure his fists would be as fragile and useless as eggshells. "Whatever happens," he told himself firmly, "Merry, Suzanne, and the Indian must not know I am afraid."

The fear that had swept over Winthrop did grow deeper the closer he came to the Indian, who stood now over Merry's small figure. It seemed to Winthrop that his feet were not moving. Only to get there, to reach Merry's side, to answer Suzanne's silent plea that he could feel pushing like a cold hand against his back!

Silverheels did not appear to notice Winthrop's approach. His eyes were on Merry, who smiled and offered

His eyes were on Merry, who offered him a scarlet leaf

him a scarlet leaf. As he bent to take it, she caught at one of his glistening braids and held to it. Silverheels seated himself on the ground and looked solemnly at her. Merry discovered the silver bangles on the moccasins and put out a hand to touch one.

"Merry?" Silverheels spoke the name inquiringly in a peculiar cadence and drew a knife from his belt.

In that moment Winthrop stood over him. Silverheels' muscles tightened slightly, but he did not hesitate. In a movement of infinite grace he cut one of the ornaments from his moccasin and dropped it into Merry's hand. Then he rose and stood towering over Winthrop.

The lad's hands trembled weakly with relief as he made the sign he recalled seeing Anselm use in greeting.

A brief interval of silence followed. Then, with an ironical smile, Silverheels spoke. "Do not have to draw air pictures. Silverheels speak the white man's tongue."

"How could this be?" thought Winthrop. The blue eyes, the English speech, the subtle smile on the savage face? "Who are you?" he managed to ask at last.

"I am Silverheels."

Still Winthrop could not guess why the Indian stood there with an air half of expectancy and half of indifference.

"What do you want?"

"I have message for you." A note of satisfaction, which seemed to have nothing to do with his statement to Winthrop, crept into Silverheels' voice. Then his expression changed to one of ancient wisdom, as if he saw all that was crowding through Winthrop's heart. "Message is from your father."

It seemed an eternity to Winthrop before he could speak. "My father?"

Silverheels nodded. "Is in my lodge." He smiled faintly. "Do not cry out. The little man is not hostage. Is only wounded."

"Take me to him!" Winthrop stepped forward eagerly.

The only answer he received was the look of withdrawal he read in Silverheels' face.

A picture began to form in Winthrop's mind. "You've been caring for him! I am grateful."

A faint light of surprise warmed the chill blue eyes. "Is enough that you are grateful. Follow me. First, send inside the gates the shy one and the little firehead *Apetotha*." Silverheels put out a hand to stop Winthrop as he turned to run up the mound. "Warn the shy one not to send soldiers after us. If they come—" He made a vicious sign.

Winthrop needed no interpreter.

Mrs. McKnight looked up from her carding to see that the sunny afternoon sky had turned bleak and was tattered with swift-moving storm clouds. She fastened her shawl about her and hastened outside the stockade to look for the girls. She should not have let them go beyond the gates, she supposed, but the day had been a good one for nutting. She peered down the road and drew her shawl closer against the chill rising wind. She hoped the children had worn their warm flannels. No use fretting, she quieted herself. Suzanne was quite a reliable young lady for her age, though given to long silences and to daydreaming about goodness knows what.

A menacing darkness slipped over the hills and settled down in the hollows. It was akin to the mood of loneliness that sometimes settled over her since the tragic death of her husband. General Putnam had been wise indeed to assign the children to her care while she was still dazed by the suddenness and the depth of her sorrow. They had helped— Suzanne, fair, forthright and steadfast, and Merry, bright and unpredictable as a wild canary. Yet, in spite of those two, there were times when old longings got the better of her good sense. How strange it would seem—and how good —to have someone's homecoming to watch for! Someone's besides the children's, that is. She pushed a lock of stray hair back under her cap. There was barely a trace of gray in it, she noted. And her hands, no longer roughened with the heavy tasks she had performed as washerwoman for the soldiers at the barracks of Fort Harmar, were really not unshapely.

"Faugh!" she said half aloud. "I am in truth getting old to have such wanderings!" With purposeful energy, she turned back toward the stockade. No respectable woman idled away the day looking down a road when there was work to be done. Before she entered the gate, she paused to look back into the woods.

Yes! That was the flutter of Suzanne's dress and the little puff of Merry's skirts! The girls were running where there was no path, heedless of the brambles that would snag their clothing. Mrs. McKnight's relief changed to annoyance. They should not find her waiting outside the gate for them. No indeed! She would be calmly about her duties when they arrived. Suzanne should patch the rips and

Merry work another line in her sampler, for punishment.

When Suzanne burst through the door, with Merry at her heels, Mrs. McKnight's reproach at their torn clothing faltered. "Merry, my child, go to the well with your little bucket. There will be someone along who will help you draw water for our supper."

But Merry was dancing with excitement. "I already know it's about Papa and that Winthrop's gone away with Silverheels."

"*What?*" Mrs. McKnight's jaw dropped.

Suzanne gave as coherent an account as possible. "Winthrop said he wouldn't be back with father for maybe a day or so," she added.

Mrs. McKnight returned automatically to her carding. That was that. She could deny no longer that she had come to let these children mean too much to her. Of course, she was glad for them, though still incapable of realizing that Merry and Suzanne would soon be gone from her. Her mind occupied itself with the many practical details that must be arranged immediately. "How many soldiers were dispatched with Winthrop to help your father comfortably down-river?"

"There was just Silverheels." The uneasiness Suzanne tried to conceal crept out.

Mrs. McKnight rose in alarm. "You mean the lad went up to that Indian's hut by canoe—two days' trip up, another two days' back—alone?"

Suzanne nodded silently, close to tears.

"La!" Mrs. McKnight bustled to the door. "Call out the militia!"

"Oh, please!" Suzanne pleaded. "Don't! You mustn't! It would spoil everything. This Indian is sort of—different. We promised on our honor that no soldiers would follow. If we go against our word—" Her voice trailed off and she shuddered, remembering Silverheels' threatening gesture.

Mrs. McKnight considered. "If not soldiers, someone else must go," she urged.

Suzanne bit her lips. "No one must go."

With Silverheels' deep strokes and Winthrop's dogged paddling, the bark canoe was borne upstream as a leaf before the gale. When darkness fell, rain came steadily. Once they stopped to empty the canoe of water and to warm themselves briefly before a fire which Silverheels managed to build out of wet twigs, as if by magic. Winthrop seized this opportunity to ask Silverheels the question uppermost in his mind. "My father—is he badly wounded?"

Silverheels looked into the fire for a long moment, as if to find there the decision whether to answer or not. "Is healed now, needs only rest," he said. He continued grudgingly, "Was drifting in bottom of canoe, Mingo arrow in his side."

"Where? At the creek mouth?"

Silverheels looked puzzled. "By what name?"

Winthrop gestured helplessly.

The Indian rose abruptly. "Was drifting where the deer cross below the otters' lodge. Silverheels know no more."

Winthrop realized he would have to be satisfied with that for the time being.

The sky began to clear shortly before dawn and the pale light of the moon wavered over the dark hills onto the water. Silverheels pointed to the rapids ahead where the moonlight broke and eddied among the moss-covered rocks, and motioned Winthrop to lay aside his paddle. With swift, feathering strokes Silverheels guided the canoe to the western shore.

Silently he led the way through the underbrush until they came in sight of his lodge. Touched with moonlight, it looked unreal to Winthrop.

Silverheels strode ahead and drew aside the deerskin over the door. "Enter," he commanded. Then he turned away.

Winthrop stepped into the pitch-black interior, his heart thudding in eagerness against his ribs. Something moved in the darkness. "Father?" He waited through the silence. Soon his eyes, more accustomed to the dark, saw it was only a blanket blowing on a peg where the wind came through the wall. He fumbled toward what looked like a pile of furs in the corner, dropped to his knees and felt along them. "Father?"

Silverheels bent to enter the doorway. The pine-knot torch in his hand sent light and shadows leaping through the room. Withrop rose. His eyes quickly scanned the hut. His father was not there! For a moment he stood empty and shaken. Then a terrible blinding rage such as he had never known seized him. "What kind of ambush is this?" he growled thickly.

Silverheels' face behind the torch turned sharp and bitter. He looked coldly and silently down at Winthrop.

Finally the lad's eyes wavered. He buried his face in his hands. Then he lifted his head; his eyes met and held Silver-heels' unflinchingly.

Silverheels stepped deep into the shadows and reached up for something. He came back to Winthrop and, in the light of the torch, held out a powder horn. It had no cap and the neck was jagged. With trembling hands Winthrop took it, felt in his pocket, and fitted the cap and broken bit of neck neatly together.

"You satisfied Father been here?" Silverheels' voice was deep as the tone of a war drum.

"Yes," Winthrop answered humbly.

"That is good. Come." The Indian motioned, torch in hand, for Winthrop to follow him outside. "*Notha* maybe strong enough to journey to Campus Martius alone." He squatted and held the torch close to the ground, searching. He rose slowly, his face savage now and distorted in the torchlight. "Silverheels' ancient foes, the Delawares, been here. Tracks show they have stolen little man. Law of tribes is, first Indian to put hand on wounded can kill, or adopt as slave or friend. Silverheels chose to make *neegah* friend." He reached out to touch the powder horn Winthrop held. "I swear on this token. Silverheels track the dishonorable Delawares, though many moons wax and wane until man you call Father and I call Friend is restored."

Winthrop, listening, gazed into Silverheels' face. He did not interrupt to question. The broken pride, the con-viction, the savage determination in the strange eyes made him believe that Silverheels spoke from the depths of his being.

And with all his soul Winthrop longed to believe that the man's vow to find Josiah would be accomplished.

"I go now, before trail dims." Silverheels' face became masklike; he turned to his hut to gather a few belongings.

Winthrop began to pace the clearing, glancing now and then at Silverheels as he passed back and forth through the screen of brush to stow weapons and several small bundles in his canoe. He wondered if Silverheels intended to set out without him to follow the still-fresh clues, but dared not ask.

At last Silverheels turned toward Winthrop and dismissed him formally, as if he scarcely saw him, "For a while our trails part." He hurled the guttering torch into the creek and turned alone through the darkness toward the river.

CHAPTER SEVEN

By the time Winthrop reached Campus Martius—weary, footsore, and disappointed—his burning anxiety for his father had given him the courage to decide to approach Governor St. Clair. It was not that he distrusted Silver-heels' intentions, but that he was determined no possibility should be overlooked in trying to hasten the rescue of his father from the wandering band of Delawares.

St. Clair was known to have more aristocratic leanings than, say, General Rufus Putnam, and was inclined to keep at a distance from the common man. Nevertheless, as Governor, it was his duty to give heed to personal problems and petitions. Winthrop was confident that Anselm, during his report on the surveyors' findings, had taken the opportunity to slip in word of Winthrop's problem. Governor St. Clair would not be entirely unprepared; he might understand his need for a prompt hearing.

Pausing only long enough to comfort Suzanne and to accept Mrs. McKnight's anxious ministration of warm bathing water, clean clothing, and scalding spice-bush tea, he entered the guard room in the southwest blockhouse and impatiently waited his turn to confer with His Excellency. There was, he noticed, also waiting for the Governor to acknowledge his presence, a plump man whose foppish grooming and gold-headed cane suggested he was not a gentleman of these parts.

Winthrop's keen eyes studied the room. A barren guard house serving as the seat of government for the whole Northwest Territory! Yet the very presence of St. Clair lent the room an air of dignity and authority. St. Clair reminded him of thin frosted glass. It wasn't the manner in which the Governor dressed, though the lace at his throat, the claret waistcoat, the fine black satin breeches, and the silver-buckled shoes were elegant. The frosted-glass quality was rather in his bearing. Another man, especially one of fifty-four, would have bent to his desk work. The Governor did not. He sat rigidly erect, bending only slightly at the neck. His face would have seemed delicate, if it had not had the sharp aquiline nose, a sudden high Scotch color, and the strong impact of deepset eyes. His finely molded mouth was primly set. Today, the imperious temper and strong will of St. Clair were visible.

The Governor nodded for the plump gentleman to take his place across the desk from him. They talked awhile in low tones. Then St. Clair's voice rose. "I can give you no promise of protection on the tract you wish to purchase until after the treaty. The successful conclusion of this treaty is the first consideration at the present. It is incredible, this delay in getting the Indian Nations to parley. The Shawnees, Delawares, and Wyandots were ready to come to council, and now, for some obscure reason, they have withdrawn."

"I understand those tribes are not easily persuaded."

St. Clair built a bridge of his fingers, and his gaze probed a dim corner. "I recall my words on the momentous day of my induction." Irony struck a flat timbre into his voice. "Endeavor to cultivate a good understanding with the natives, without too much familiarity. Treat them upon all occasions with kindness and with the strictest regard to justice. Run not into their customs and habits, which is but too frequently the case with those who settle near them; but endeavor to induce them to adopt yours. They will soon become sensible of the superior advantages of a state of civilization."

The bridge collapsed. "Ha! What has it come to? We walk on tiptoe for fear of displeasing them. Our women deprive their families of food so the red men may feast!"

"His Excellency is wise in refusing me, now." The stranger spoke softly. "In view of your remote situation it is best to coddle these savages for awhile. Should you call down the howling pack on yourselves by any rash action, you would be corpses before Congress or the Secretary of War learned of your plight."

"Or stirred from their plush seats to send us aid, more Federal troops at Fort Harmar." The Governor sniffed. "Bah! Undesirables! Hirelings! And the militia?" he asked bitterly. "The militia knows little of soldiering, is not dependable, lacks discipline."

Winthrop squirmed on the bench. Surely, the Governor was not aware of his presence or he would not speak so freely. His gout must be uncommonly bad this morning! Obviously, this was not the hour to present his request, urgent though it was. He rose to leave.

St. Clair looked up sharply. "You might as well remain, young man, and listen. I am weary of mincing words behind closed doors. It would be better if everyone realized our situation."

The crack of rifle fire from the vicinity of the river brought St. Clair, unmindful of his gout, to the window. His severe expression deepened. A large dugout of Indians was making toward Fort Harmar, white flag hoisted, pausing between swift strokes to send a running fire into the air. He turned away as he heard the dull report of the three-volley salute and the faint quaver of fifes as the soldiers of Fort Harmar piped the savages ashore.

"One could not find a more genteel gathering than the proprietors of the Ohio Company 'to bring the beautiful fabric of civilized life to perfection,' if I may borrow from Your Excellency's address," the man remarked soothingly, and made a great show of seating the Governor comfortably again at his desk.

The black brows eased, then pinched together. "Yet I have a feeling they are going against me. And for a man of property and intelligence to be tinged with democracy is a crime against our class. Furthermore, in the Territory the majority would rather farm than fight. And I say the British will have the Indians at our throats before we can move to prevent it. Yes!" St. Clair thumped the table. "It is the British who are behind this delay in the treaty! But I can't put my finger on the means by which they are accomplishing it." He pushed back his chair to rise. A twinge of pain twisted his lips. "If you will excuse me, we shall continue our interview on the morrow."

St. Clair watched the man until he was out of the door. "Drat the fellow!" He sighed irritably. "He didn't set so well with my nerves." He turned in his chair and cautiously extended his feet so that contact with the floor was less painful. "Now, young man, what brings you here?"

Winthrop's ears were still tingling. The Governor's tirade had reduced to almost nothing his hope of military help in the search for his father. "It was only a private matter, sir. Some other time when Your Excellency is in better spirits—" His voice stammered into embarrassed silence under St. Clair's ironical scrutiny.

"So?" The Governor raised his eyebrows and looked at Winthrop for a long moment. Then he spoke with a hint of sadness. "Do not mistake my firmness for harshness. The land speculator who just left has no respect for governmental virtues, no wish to build cities and bring culture to this forest land. All he wants is money from the land on which he will probably never set foot, at the cost of the lives of those who must defend it."

"Yes, sir," Winthrop agreed politely and backed toward the doorway.

"Oh, come now!" St. Clair smiled thinly. "My temper isn't that bad. But let us go to my quarters to discuss this private matter before some dolt comes in to further agitate me."

Winthrop followed St. Clair's limping lead. With one part of his mind he was trying to form a new plan that would not irritate His Excellency. With another, he wondered that the Governor's temper was not even shorter, what with the gout, his family not yet there to comfort him, his people set against his laws, the failure at the Falls, and now the new delay in the treaty.

It was rumored that if St. Clair failed as Governor of the Northwest Territory, for which appointment he had left his post as President of the Continental Congress, General Washington's favor would not withstand this final test. True, the old Continental Congress of the thirteen colonies had outlived its usefulness, and some thought St. Clair's post in the wilderness was intended as a stepping-stone toward a high political future with the new Federal government-to-be. Others remembered Governor St. Clair for his military misfortune in losing Ticonderoga to the British in New York. Washington had not blamed him personally, and St. Clair, demanding an official inquiry into the circumstances of his defeat, had been exonerated. Still, gossips whispered that he was a weak general, cowardly, even treacherous. The situation here at Campus Martius was similar, though on a smaller scale, to that at Ticonderoga. The forces at St. Clair's command were far too few and too ill-prepared, should war with the Indians come.

Winthrop started to ask himself what, after all, he was doing in the presence of a man of such distinction as General—now Governor—St. Clair. Then the sense of urgency overcame his shyness. When the Governor bade him enter and be seated on the low stool by the fireplace, he sat looking about the room, trying to quell his impatience until it was His Excellency's pleasure to speak.

St. Clair sat erect in his high-backed chair and methodically measured a pinch of snuff. The muscles of his face relaxed slightly. "Now, what is this private matter?"

"Now, what is this private matter?"

Winthrop summoned his courage again. He decided it was best to be forthright. "It is about my father, sir. Josiah Lake."

St. Clair went through the file of his memory. "Oh, yes! You are his son, Winthrop. Mrs. McKnight is befriending your sisters. You have news of your father?"

The question hung in the air. Finally, Winthrop told him of his trip to Silverheels' lodge. He watched St. Clair's face as he concluded. "I believe that Silverheels is honorable, that he told me the truth. I believe my father is now a captive of the Delawares."

The Governor considered this a while in silence, weighing the odds. When he spoke, his voice was cautious.

"Silverheels has been a particular problem to our spies. Because he is a half-breed, his loyalties are divided. Once we sent a small intelligence party of soldiers to observe his activities. He routed them in such a manner that none can be persuaded to volunteer again. On the other hand, he has been known to be capable of deep attachments to those settlers who have treated him with respect."

Winthrop squirmed on his stool. He knew all this. Was the Governor playing for time, trying to evade the issue?

"As to the Delawares," St. Clair continued, "yes, there was a party in that vicinity. You will recall I ordered a halt to the surveying activities—" He paused, then added with significant emphasis "—to forestall any trouble that would endanger their coming early to treaty."

The emphasis was not lost on Winthrop. He understood now it was completely hopeless to expect St. Clair to send an immediate rescue party. A wave of indignation swept over him. A sense of helplessness turned to futile anger. A man's life meant nothing against a precious treaty!

A shadow fell across St. Clair's face as he appeared to read Winthrop's thoughts. "You are young, lad, and impetuous. Please have the patience to hear me through. A rescue party would be a death warrant for your father, possibly for many others. As a captive, if such he is, he has more than a good chance. If he conducts himself peaceably and bides his time, our time to act will come."

"Sir, please know that I cannot stand by without lifting a hand." Witnhrop tried to keep his voice level.

"There are more experienced hands—and heads—at this business." St. Clair spoke mildly. "A detachment from Fort

Harmar is going downriver to Vincennes shortly. That is a strategic spot for receiving and dispatching quick intelligence. I shall inform them regarding your father. They will be especially on the alert."

"Thank you, sir." Winthrop attempted to conceal his disappointment.

"In the meantime, since the season has grown so late, with winter bearing down upon us, there is no longer hope of conducting treaty negotiations in a bowery of green leaves and branches; a Council House is being constructed near the fort. Would it not be wiser and safer for all interests if you were to help to build it? There you might learn much. I shall instruct Monsieur La Chapelle, my interpreter, to aid you."

The Governor's pointed gaze signified to Winthrop that his suggestion was in reality an order. He rose from his stool, touched his hand in salute, and turned away.

St. Clair's voice followed him to the door. "Please believe I wish you well. And by the way, I'd wager that in this matter Silverheels might accomplish more than a platoon of my militia."

CHAPTER EIGHT

Suzanne did not need to lift the lid of the kettle to know there would be fish again for dinner. This time there would be no sauce, nor even salt, to alter the too familiar taste. She swung the crane closer to the fire and went to the window to watch for Winthrop's return from the Council House. She saw little more of him these days, except at meal time, than when he had been with the surveyors. Now and then she caught an extra glimpse of him as he drove an ox-load of timber from the saw pits, or crossed the river between Fort Harmar and Campus Martius on errands for the construction crew. He worked with a dogged steadiness that made him almost a stranger to her. But then, was she not doing the same? She was almost a stranger to herself!

She and Mrs. McKnight, it seemed, spent their days in endless duties and in weighing, planning, and managing somehow to keep themselves and their neighbors from constant hunger. Mrs. McKnight's larder had been better stocked than most, but her generosity had so reduced it— especially as new boatloads of families arrived, totally unprepared for the frontier scarcity of provisions—that she, like the others, was never certain what the next fare would be. Perhaps it was just as well to be occupied with the day-to-day problems. Often Suzanne was too tired to lie awake at night, desperately praying for her father's safety and listening to the creak and groan of the forest in which she knew he was.

Winter had closed down with a vicious snap. Now, as she stood at the window looking toward Fort Harmar, the wind swooped from the hills, flung snow upon the Muskingum, and swelled up the bank in immense swirls that foamed against the outer pickets of the stockade. Still no sign of her brother. But there was something to occupy her hands and mind; there was pumpkin bread to be made.

Carefully she scraped the sides of the crock and measured a spoon of lard into the dry mixture. Every family had been advised to use lard sparingly since the last four of the community's hogs had rooted their way out under the brush pen, wandered to the forest, and been eaten by wolves. Fortunate wolves! Suzanne thought wryly. It had been six weeks now since any one in the colony had tasted meat. Perhaps now that the labor of building the Council House was done, the company might see fit to slaughter an ox. Or, with good luck, a hunter might bring in a deer. No one dared complain, with every peaceable effort being made to entice the tribes to treaty, that it was the Indians who had driven off or destroyed all the game within a radius of twenty miles. Nor did anyone dare to gaze hungrily at the storeroom in the northeast blockhouse that contained each family's contribution toward the feast that was to celebrate the conclusion of the treaty.

It was not due to lack of foresight that the settlement wanted for provisions. Who could have foretold the early October frost that seared the corn while still in the milk, so that even the cattle sickened from eating it? Was it Rufus Putnam's fault that the Upper Ohio was ice-bound and no boats with provisions could come through? Or that the good neighbor, Isaac Williams, could no longer provide emergency supplies from his little plantation across on the Virginia side of the Ohio?

No! Suzanne straightened, cheeks flushed from the fire and from a sense of guilt that had deepened every time she watched Mrs. McKnight share her meager hoard. It was the fault of Suzanne and Winthrop Lake that the colony went hungry! Fifty sacks of meal were on their flatboat. What if it was all they owned with which to make a new start in Kentucky? Kentucky seemed very far away, these days. She hurried again to the window, even more impatient for Winthrop's return.

Mrs. McKnight came from the bedroom, raised the kettle lid, and sniffed in distaste. She bent to prod the pumpkin bread with an impatient finger. "In my lifetime, I thought there were but four kinds of bread," she said, sighing. "Cornbread baked on a board before the fire. Biscuits browned over coals in the Dutch oven. Clay bread raised in the small clay oven. Or stone bread, baked as we baked it in New England, many loaves at once in the great heated stone or brick oven. Hardtack of the soldiers' rations does not count. Now we have a fifth—pumpkin bread, if bread it be. Faugh! I call it a tasteless substitute."

Suzanne looked around with a smile at Widow McKnight, knowing her blustering was really an apology. "We fare well enough."

"We manage," the woman corrected. "When the first boat arrives after the thaw you shall have stone bread, loaves of it, lest you forget how civilized folk eat."

"Bread?" The word caught Merry's attention. She came from the corner where she had been singing in a monotone to her rag doll and looked up at Mrs. McKnight, her small red tongue licking around her lips hungrily.

"Land sakes! What have I been saying?" Mrs. McKnight muttered to herself. "In time, child." She patted Merry's copper curls.

"Milk?" Merry pursued.

"Last week you had milk," Mrs. McKnight reminded her patiently. "This week it is another child's turn."

"Maple sugar?" Merry pointed hopefully to the covered bowl on the cupboard shelf.

"When spring comes, and we can boil the sap in the big kettle."

"When spring comes, bread and milk and sugar!" Merry made a little song of it and skipped back to her corner, satisfied for the time being.

Suzanne turned again to the window. "Tomorrow," she was vowing to herself, "there'll be corn bread for all."

Shortly before midday, Suzanne ran to open the door for Winthrop. He entered, stamping snow from his boots and letting in a gust of frosty air.

"Down to our last sticks of firewood, and we should try to heat the wilderness!" Mrs. McKnight scolded. "A good thing the wilderness is full of more firewood for the asking and the cutting. Close the door and hand me your coat before it drips puddles on the clean floor."

Winthrop stood, instead, with hands behind him and he grinned rakishly. "What's cooking in yonder pot?"

"Your nose tells you and you know very well it is fish!" she answered tartly.

"Throw it back in the river!" Winthrop said grandly, and with a flourish brought from behind his back a brace of ducks and three squirrels.

Mrs. McKnight gasped. She stood there for a moment unable to say a word.

Suzanne's heart lifted more in gratitude for the return of Winthrop's high spirits than for the game. "How did you come by them?" she asked, watching with admiration as he crossed the room to lay the game on the puncheon table, his stiff leather breeches wheezing at every step.

"By trade," Winthrop answered airily. "With Chippewa squaws coming in to set up camp for their men-folk."

"What could a body value more than this?" Mrs. McKnight stroked a plump mallard breast wonderingly.

"Just an old belt." Winthrop shrugged.

"Not your braided horsehair with the silver buckle?" Suzanne asked, aghast.

Winthrop tightened the rawhide thong about his waist. "This serves just as well."

Mrs. McKnight tore her gaze from the ducks and squirrels. "I'll have no part of any victuals bought at the cost of a keepsake."

Winthrop studiously ignored her discomfort. "See that they're cooked to a turn," he teased.

She compressed her lips, but a smile escaped over the little paths at the corners of her eyes.

"Now for the big news!" Winthrop teetered important-
ly on his toes. "The sentry says the tribes are less than a
mile up the Muskingum, on their way to the Council House.
The troops at Fort Harmar have been called to dress parade
and already our delegation from Campus Martius is forming
for welcome."

"Glory be for this day of December thirteenth!" the
woman exclaimed fervently.

"Listen!" he exclaimed.

A bugle fanfare sounded. Winthrop flung open the
door leading to the courtyard. All along the four sides of the
inner wall other doors banged open, shutters creaked, and
the murmur of excited voices rose.

"Here comes Governor St. Clair!" someone shouted.

A guard of honor bore a large chair on which was
seated Arthur St. Clair, so ailing with the gout that he
could not walk from the sally port toward the main gate
of the outer fortifications opening onto the Muskingum. St.
Clair sat erect. The blue of his coat was deeper than the
sky, suddenly swept clear of its snow flurries. His sword and
epaulettes glittered more spendidly than the sun. Following
him on foot, saber drawn, was the always elegantly attired
Winthrop Sargent, Secretary of the Territory. Next, in
worn military uniforms, came the judges of the court, General Putnam, General Benjamin Tupper, and Colonel Archi-
bald Crary. A few of the onlookers noted, with sadness, the
absence of another judge, General James Mitchell Varnum.
It was he who had delivered a great patriotic oration at the
settlement's Fourth of July celebration. Now he lay on his
deathbed in the upper chamber of a house at the Point.

The military officers and dignitaries of the company followed, according to their rank. Walking humbly at the rear, in worn clerical robes, hands piously folded, was the Reverend John Heckewelder, busy Moravian missionary who was beloved by even the more warlike tribes.

Winthrop scooped Merry into his arms and made a way for Suzanne and Mrs. McKnight through the crowd that closed around the last of the procession. "This way!" he called and clambered up the dim stairway to the belfry tower that capped the northwest blockhouse. They reached the outlook just in time to watch St. Clair and his party embark in the *Congress,* the huge official barge sent over from Fort Harmar for the purpose. They watched its rapid progress for the short distance downriver, sped on by twelve oarsmen in white uniforms and caps. Soon the fifty-two-foot barge reached its destination. Its passengers disembarked and wound in a little procession up the bank toward the gleaming, newly built log Council House just outside the northeast bastion of the fort.

Then from the other direction, from far up the Muskingum, a ribbon of color threaded in and out of the dip and swell of the western bank. Gradually it widened and thickened. Spearheading the column was a lone horseman carrying the unfurled flag of the "Thirteen Fires," the United States. As the column drew nearer, Winthrop pointed out the various tribes represented in a voice hushed with awe. "The Ohio Miamis, Wyandots, and Delawares; Chippewas and Ottawas from the shores of Lake Michigan; Senecas from the East. There must be at least two hundred Indian braves!"

"There must be two hundred Indian braves!"

Mrs. McKnight sighed as she watched. "I'd like to have some of those scarlets for my patchwork quilt."

"I think they have decked themselves out in all those ornaments to hide their fear of us." Suzanne spoke thoughtfully.

Merry stood on tiptoe. "Is Silverheels there?"

Winthrop shook his head. "The Shawnees have refused to take part in the treaty. But even if they hadn't, little Merry, Silverheels would not be among them."

"Poor Silverheels!" Merry cried dramatically. "To miss all this fun!"

As the parade came opposite Campus Martius, the Indians paused and fired their guns into the air in token of friendship. Then a military guard came marching forth from Fort Harmar, smart in blue and buff, to meet the blanketed, trinketed natives' cavalcade and form an escort for it. Army musicians struck up a lively tune and the procession moved onward. Once more the Indians loaded and fired their muskets. This time the salute was answered by the sullen ga-boom! of cannon and the crack of musketry from the soldiers remaining at Fort Harmar. For several minutes the hills echoed with the deafening, rattling sounds. Winthrop was surprised to hear himself shouting along with the others. With difficulty he remembered this was a salute to peace.

All normal affairs of the settlement were suspended for the balance of the day. The holiday spirit touched even the busy housewives. Mrs. McKnight settled herself in the seldom-used homemade rocking chair by the fire, for once content to sit with idle hands. "Now we may look for progress," she pronounced with satisfaction. "When spring comes we may cultivate the outlots in peace, fence the communal fields, erect the mill at Waterford, and survey the rest of the Donation tract. When the new road is cut from Alexandria on the Potomac to the Ohio River opposite the Point, we shall see wagonloads of stores the year round. "Now," she concluded, "we may build instead of brawl."

Suzanne stole a glance at Winthrop as he sat at the table, a generous portion of roast duck still on his plate. He stared into the fire, the strange quietness upon him again. "By the first article of the treaty as they expect to have it drawn," he said, thinking aloud, "the tribes are to give up all white prisoners in their hands to Governor St. Clair at Fort Harmar."

Mrs. McKnight's rocker creaked to a standstill. "Heaven forgive me. And I was talking about supplies."

Suzanne half rose from her bench. "How long must we wait?" she asked breathlessly.

"Who knows?" Her brother sighed. "The treaty could drag on for weeks." He rose abruptly, went to his greatcoat and returned with two squares of rawhide. "You need a new pair of brogues," he remarked gruffly.

Mrs. McKnight looked at the fair braids swinging over the dark head as Winthrop placed Suzanne's foot on one square of the hide with the hair side up, cut it round, gathered the sides upon her instep and secured them by a whang of thong leather. Something made Mrs. McKnight decide to leave them alone. She put on her shawl, took Merry by the hand, and before the child knew what was happening, they were outside.

Now was the moment, Suzanne thought, to bring up the subject of the meal on their boat. While Winthrop sat on the floor to make the second brogue, she planned her approach. "When Father comes—" she carefully emphasized *when* "—you can give a good accounting of yourself. You've helped at surveying, building the Council House—"

"I haven't helped," Winthrop protested abruptly as he cut a gash in the rawhide. "It is we who have been helped and have given nothing in return."

Suzanne sank down on the bench and looked at him a long moment. Yes, the guilt of having and not sharing had been weighing on him, too. "You traded your belt for food," she reminded mildly.

Winthrop measured another length of the whang before he spoke. "That's not worth mentioning." He seemed about to go on, then hesitated.

Suzanne sat very still.

"On our boat are fifty sacks of meal," he blurted, looking up at her with a gaze of near-defiance.

"Enough to see the colony through the winter." Suzanne appeared to think of it for the first time.

"And to help at the council feast!" Winthrop's eyes brightened. Then he shook his head as if to clear it.

"What, though, if Father returned to find the meal gone?" she asked.

Winthrop rose and paced the floor. After a while he stood still and said with a quiet smile, "I think he'd call us both idiots—and worse—if he found the meal mouldering there on the boat while our neighbors and ourselves are half starving."

"We could sell it," Suzanne ventured.

"Sell it?" Winthrop echoed in scorn. "It's worth four times its value when we milled it!" His face reddened. "Such a price I could not ask of friends. First I would rather see it in the bottom of the river."

"General Putnam would rather see it in the storehouse," Suzanne suggested softly.

Winthrop's face lit with a smile. "That's what I've been waiting all along for you to say!"

Suzanne was speechless with astonishment. Then each, seeing the other's guile, broke into laughter.

Rufus Putnam did not return from the Council House until evening. He had removed his boots and settled to nurse his pipe reflectively when Winthrop, followed by Suzanne, rapped at his door. Though he was tired and vaguely annoyed as he crossed the room, his face eased into friendly welcome as he saw them at the stone doorstep. "Come in, come in!" He held the door wide. "It is good of you to call on a lonely old man. I was just wishing for my family."

Suzanne glanced about the unfinished room. It did look lonely and unlived in.

"As soon as this place is finished as I have designed it, or mayhap even before, I'll go back to Massachusetts and conduct them here myself. My wife, two sons, six daughters, and two little grandchildren."

"They will like it here," Suzanne murmured politely.

Winthrop shuffled his feet in embarrassment. Now that he was about to offer the meal he wondered how to do so without seeming to make a grand gesture of it.

General Putnam noted that they were both ill at ease. "There, now, so long I've been in the wilderness I've near forgot my manners! Let me help you with your cloak, Suzanne. And you, Winthrop, give me your coat."

The two stood in silence while Putnam hung their wraps in a small closet.

"Since you've been engaged in building the Council House, would you like to see the details of construction here?" the man suggested to Winthrop.

"Well, sir, we really came on a sort of business—" Winthrop faltered, then seized gratefully on the familiar subject. "The Council House is crude compared with this. Through the roof and sides you can see enough sky to cut a Dutchman a pair of breeches." He grinned, comfortable again. "Your quarters look completely defensible."

"So they should be!" Putnam nodded with gruff pleasure. "With the hours I spent working out details, they should be worthy." He showed him a drafting of the mortise-and-tenon construction.

Suzanne soon wearied of their talk. She began to move restlessly about the room. A half-open closet door at the side of the huge stone fireplace attracted her notice. She peered in. The emptiness of it extended up and up. She drew back quickly and Putnam hurried over to explain. "Here a shaft will lead up to the second story. Fitted with a system of weights and pulleys, it will slowly turn the spit and roast my meats evenly before a roaring fire!" He beamed at his ingenuity. "A pity I cannot offer you a taste this very minute," he added ruefully.

Winthrop suddenly remembered their errand. "Oh,

sir! We know how everyone is pressed for supplies. My sister and I want you to take the grist from our flat boat."

"Well, now," Putnam peered at them earnestly, "what is your price?"

"We want no profit from those who have befriended us all these months," Winthrop said firmly.

"We don't want anything." Suzanne's clear gaze met the General's.

"Ho! What kind of business is this?"

"My father would offer it at far below the present market price if he were here—just as a miller passing down-river," Winthrop answered. "But because of your kindness to us, I do not doubt he would give it to you outright. We would like to do the same."

General Putnam scratched his chin reflectively. "I cannot take your security and offer none in return." He pondered awhile in silence. "Suppose I have legal papers drawn to the effect that when your father returns the company will pay him any price he demands. In the event he does not return—"

"There will be no such event," Winthrop cut in shortly.

The General was not one to express emotion, but Winthrop read in his face deep regret for having spoken his doubt as to Josiah's safety, and a gratitude beyond words.

General Putnam drew chairs for them into the encircling warmth of the fire. He talked on into the night of the affairs of the settlement. Never had Winthrop and Suzanne felt so honored.

CHAPTER NINE

Through the remaining days of December and into the new year of 1789, smoke rose from the council fire in a towering column. Every morning St. Clair was borne in his chair from Campus Martius to sit white-faced and unflinching through the ceremonious exchange of speechmaking that droned on and on, first in English, then as interpreted to the tribal leaders. Still there was little progress and no decision.

"After all," Anselm reminded Winthrop one morning as they lounged outside the bastion of Fort Harmar awaiting news of the proceedings, "it is no small thing St. Clair is trying to accomplish." He drew a quick sketch in the snow. "By renewing the treaty of Fort Stanwix, the Indians are giving up all claim to this huge swath of land from Niagara on Lake Ontario, to the portage between Lakes Erie and Ontario, to the northern boundary of Pennsylvania, and down along its western line to the Ohio."

"Some bargain in exchange for three thousand dollars in goods!" Winthrop muttered. "But what is holding up this second treaty, with the tribes in our own territory? The exchange seems more fair."

Anselm's eyebrows rose. "You think so? On the surface, yes. Actually, it restrains the tribes from keeping a foothold eastward beyond the Cuyahoga-Tuscarawas-Miami River district bounded on the north by Lake Erie. Cornplanter, the Chief of the Senecas, although in general very friendly toward the white settlers, can foresee in it the day the Indians will be forced to abandon the Ohio Valley— their 'beloved bear grounds'—completely."

Winthrop's thought went back to the afternoon on the river when his father had explained, "It is one thing to be agreeable to half-understood promises written on paper, another to be driven from your homeland." He sat awhile in silence listening to the voice of Monsieur La Chapelle as it came through the thin walls of the Council House, rising and falling in the melodious cadences of the Delaware tongue. Then he turned to Anselm and asked, "What if the Indians refuse to sign?"

"Don't forget that St. Clair's mind makes up in nimbleness for his gout-crippled legs," was the answer. "Also, it is necessary for him personally that the treaty be brought to an early and successful conclusion. He wants to be getting over to New York by March, to be present when the new Federal Government becomes a reality. Everyone supposes that General Washington will be the choice of the electoral college, for President of the United States—but it's only now, this first Wednesday of January, that the electors themselves are being chosen! Unless I miss my guess, General St. Clair will have the treaty signed within a fortnight."

"He is a rare man!" Winthrop exclaimed appreciatively. "Even with all his troubles, he hasn't forgotten mine. Remember, I told you last week he sent a messenger for me? In his office I saw the report of the spies working out from Post Vincent. It said there was a white man with a band of Delawares hunting along the Great Miami."

Anselm, though he had heard Winthrop's account pre-
viously, knew his need to talk. He encouraged him, "So the
Governor—?"

"St. Clair even let me be present as he questioned the
Delaware chief, old Captain Pipes, through La Chapelle.
The interpreter said that the white man with the Delaware
hunters was a British trader, not a captive. La Chapelle told
me afterward he'd queried enough other Indians to be confident that Captain Pipes was telling the truth." He rose in a
fit of restlessness that often came over him. "No message at
all from Silverheels. His lodge has been empty since Fall.
Our scouts report no trace of him."

Anselm unfolded his lanky length and put a hand on
Winthrop's shoulder. "Take heart! There'll be news when
you least expect it."

One forenoon, a few days later, when Winthrop was
chopping wood on the windy ridge above Fort Harmar, he
heard the cannon thud across the frosty air. Axe poised, he
stood still to count the reports. Thirteen! The signal that the
treaty had been signed! He buried the axe-head deep in a
stump, ignored the long trail, and made his way down the
face of the cliff, holding to scrub growth, and sliding along a
gully. He ran across a furrowed field, past the pickets, and
through the main gate which now stood open.

The parade ground was already filled with a murmuring
crowd such as gathers for a great occasion or a great calami-
ty. Uniformed soldiers hurried in and out of the gate. Men
from Campus Martius, in their sober work clothes, talked
excitedly with officers in flowing capes. A few buckskin-clad
trappers wandered about, looking lonely even in the press of

the crowd. Indians in quickly assumed ceremonial dress swarmed everywhere in a confusion of color, and the drone of their strange language rose over all.

Six soldiers marched out of the barracks drumming the muster-call, making an aisle through the throng. The military officers in their buff and blue uniforms drew together into a formal line, and across the small space the chieftains ranked themselves in glittering splendor. Into the aisle of space walked La Chapelle, a lone figure in the simple dress of a woodsman, a swarthy, deep-chested man with long black hair plaited Shawnee style. The murmur of the crowd sank into silence as he unfurled a parchment before him.

"On this day of January ninth, 1789," he read in ringing tones, "you are requested to inform the Wyandots, Delawares, Chippewas, Ottawas, Miamis, Potawatomis, and Sacs, with the Senecas and such of the Five Nations as are present, that we are desirous of celebrating the good work which the Great Spirit has permitted our father, the Governor, and the sachems and chiefs so happily to accomplish; for which purpose we will prepare entertainment on Monday next, at two o'clock." He turned and bowed low to the chieftains who stood in solemn attention.

He read on. "Our brothers, the sachems and chiefs to whom we now send tokens, are requested to attend at that time that we may in friendship and as true brothers eat and drink together and smoke the pipe of everlasting peace; and evince to the whole world how bright and strong is the chain which the thirteen United States hold fast at one end, and our great native tribes hold at the other."

He paused, his dark eyes sweeping beyond the chieftains to the dark-skinned women gathered humbly behind them. "We are very sorry that we cannot entertain all our brethren together with their wives and children; but as we have come into this country a very long way, some of us forty or fifty days' journey from land toward the rising sun, and could not bring much provision along with us, it is now out of our power. We trust the Great Spirit will permit us to plant and gather our corn, and increase our stores, and that their children and children's children may be told how much we shall all rejoice to make glad their hearts when they come to see us."

La Chapelle turned to repeat the invitation in the liquid syllables of the wilderness people. His voice took on a different quality. In it Winthrop heard the murmur of green rivers. He thought of forest haunts where deer bedded in ferns. He remembered hills over which the sunset flowed and drowned in misty hollows. He saw again sun on wide bottomlands rippling with corn. And he felt pity for the silent Indians. An invitation to dinner was little enough in return for these things.

The women of Marietta were not concerned with the intricacies of the treaty. That it had been concluded was enough. It meant peace and the end of daily anxiety. It promised the long-awaited celebration with a New England dinner followed by wine, tobacco, and speeches. The doors of the storehouse were thrown open and the good ladies filed in and out, each to bear a small treasure back to her own fireplace. Suzanne was reminded of a colony of industrious ants. Soon from the chimneys—many of them still unfinished—billowed columns of smoke, while the seventy-two rooms of Campus Martius—though many of them, too, were unfinished and unoccupied—began smelling of cooking delicacies.

Mrs. McKnight's supervision of her kitchen was equal to that of any general of maneuvers. "Suzanne," she ordered, "put the corn to soak for the making of hominy, then come help me stir this bowl of meal." She looked up with a smile, arms dusted with gold to the elbows. "Indeed, nowhere have I seen the quality of this meal. You and Winthrop have done more than your Christian duty to provide it for the settlement."

"We should have done it long ago," Suzanne answered modestly, though she blushed with pleasure. She set the kettle of corn to soak and went to turn the haunch of venison on the spit. "Now, if only we had salt!"

The woman's nostrils quivered. "If only there's a taste of the meat left for us after we are done serving, I'll not ask for salt!" She turned her attention from the mixing bowl to the activities across the square. "From the look of the chimneys over there, the Cushings' roast, the Nyes' puddings, the Meigs's sauce, and the Olneys' turnips will be ruined if their men don't get home with more firewood within the hour. If you can't find Winthrop at once, go to the hall and ask one of the gentlemen setting up tables to fetch some into the square." She followed Suzanne to the door, spoon in hand, adding, "When you do find Winthrop set him to work also at the hominy block."

Suzanne traced the sounds of gay tobogganers to the slide on Sacra Via outside the northern curtain of the garrison. There the ancient approach from the Muskingum to the elevated mounds was packed slick as ice between the parallel earthen ramps. Yes, there was Winthrop, the one in the coonskin hat, leading the group just clearing the top of the hill. She watched while he swung the Indian snow toboggan around, lifted the nose by its bark twine rope, looked to make sure the boys behind him each had a firm foothold on the long, narrow strip of white elm bark placed smooth side down.

"We're off!" he shouted, and away they went, gaining speed until they shot out onto the level frozen river.

Suzanne sat on the snowy bank and waited for Winthrop to return. She wished she did not have to call him from his sledding. It was not good that he had no time for winter sports as other boys had. For months he had been doing a man's work. As a matter of fact, she had come to look upon him as the head of the household, even as Merry had begun to come to him for the little services that had been Father's special duty.

As Winthrop trudged up the grade, he caught sight of Suzanne and began to run. "Hello, Susu!" His cheeks glowed and his dark eyes flashed merrily. "Want to try it?"

Suzanne clapped her hands. "It would be like flying!" Then she remembered her errand. "Maybe after the banquet. But right now, some of the ladies are needing wood. Do you mind hauling in a supply from the rick outside the sally port? Then there's hominy to be pounded in the block."

Winthrop's smile became a grimace of mingled disappointment and resentment. But without a word he pushed the toboggan down the mound toward the boys.

Suzanne stole a glance at him from under her hood as

they walked along the path under the jutting northwest blockhouse. She walked in silence, her face composed lest she should put him in further ill humor. But her heart yearned to tell him that she, too, knew the yoke of responsibility did not set easily.

They stopped to watch a group of women haggling with a trader. The roughly dressed fellow was demanding that his decrepit, burdened packhorse, harnessed to a sled crudely but sturdily built for travel over snow and mud alike, should be admitted to the square before he would show his wares.

"No wagons or carts are permitted," one housewife flatly stated while trying to peer under the sled's cover.

"Or horses, cattle, or swine allowed to be fed inside the square," another recited religiously from the rules.

"No cattle or swine?" The trader cackled. "What about all the Injuns I hear your menfolk are to feed with here, this afternoon?"

Before Suzanne could stop him, Winthrop had the trader by the collar of his racoon coat and was shaking him unmercifully, growling, "Hold your tongue!"

The women fell back with distressed little shrieks as the tremendous figure of the settlement's sheriff, Colonel Ebenezer Sproat, bore down on the gathering. It was for good reason the Indians had dubbed him *Hetuck*, or Big Buck Eye. Now his glare was fixed on Winthrop.

"Disturbing the peace on this day of brotherhood!" he rumbled. "From the directors' office above, I saw you attack this poor man without warning. Unloose him at once!"

"Sir, I was only trying to—" Winthrop began, abashed.

"This is not a court! You will defend yourself properly —if you can—when the next session sits. Mr. Backus—" he summoned his young deputy who was standing nearby— "see that a warrant is made out and served at the proper time. He need not be confined in jail. He will be more useful continuing as a helper for Mrs. McKnight and filling in on tasks General Putnam assigns him—"

"But because of his youth, sir—" James Backus began.

"Old enough to assault a poor peddler, he's old enough to stand trial like a man." Sproat dismissed that matter and turned to the trembling trader. "You! Just what is your business here?"

The trader snatched off his cap and bowed. "Food, yer honor. Bear meat. A bit of the summer's wild honey." Then with a dramatic gesture he pointed to the bundles of husks under the boards of his forked pack saddle. "Salt!"

"Salt!" echoed Colonel Sproat, his barrel chest expanding. "Salt would be the very making of our feast, so long we've been without it! Well, haul your wares around to the main gate where all may see. Take care that all is priced and portioned fairly." He turned gallantly to the ladies. "Spread the good word around. If there be those who have not time to dig their crock of hard cash from under the floor or wherever, I'm certain the Ohio Company will advance what is necessary." He strode pompously away.

Winthrop stood alone, forgotten even by the trader, who guided his sled and ungainly packhorse toward the main gate, and by the women who trailed after him. But Suzanne came up to her brother and timidly touched his arm. "You should feel better now," she ventured wisely.

111

Winthrop's scowl eased as he looked down at her. "You're right. At least I came up against something solid for a change!"

"Still, I can't figure why I challenged him," he went on later while Suzanne poured the grain into the burned-out hollow of a tree stump, serving as a hominy block near the saw pits. He raised the sapling bough at the end of which swung the wooden pestle, and brought it down sharply.

Suzanne silently ladled a gourd of samp from the block into an iron pot of water and skimmed the hulls and chaff from the top.

"Maybe I was remembering the Indians' faces when La Chapelle read the invitation to the feast," Winthrop went on. He brought the pestle down again and again, rhythmically. "Maybe I was remembering that Silverheels cared for Father." The long sweep wavered uncertainly. "Yet—why should I take up for a people who may be holding Father as a slave this very minute?"

"You did right." Suzanne spoke with gentle firmness.

"I hope the next session of court sees it that way," he said ruefully, and brought the pestle down until the last of the grain was crushed.

That afternoon, the Indians and the officials of Campus Martius, dignitaries from the Point, and the officers of Fort Harmar sat at the long tables after the last platter had been removed, puffing their tobacco and sipping their wine. Suzanne and the serving women had left the hall and were huddled in the doorway. Winthrop sat on a stool in a dim corner awaiting the signal from St. Clair to refill the glasses for another toast.

Suzanne poured the grain into the burned-out hollow of a tree stump

Cornplanter lifted his hand in greeting

Cornplanter rose, lifted his hand in greeting, and the room subsided into respectful silence. Cornplanter was magnificent in his humiliation, brave in the face of his people's scorn of appeasement as the only way to survive. His black eyes were quiet with patience and dignity. A tiny metal pendant hung from the thin ring that pierced his long nose; it barely swung as he spoke. His headdress was of wrought metal, sprouting a large clustered topknot of feathers that nodded slightly to each other, now and then. On his wrists he wore heavy metal bands and, suspended on a chain around his neck, was a brass epaulette, probably a trophy from some encounter with the colonists. His colorful robes were draped in graceful folds.

In Cornplanter's voice as he spoke were sorrow, disdain, wisdom, and a calm integrity. "I thank the Great Spirit for this opportunity of smoking the pipe of friendship and love. May we plant our own vines and maintain them."

While Cornplanter continued his speech, Silverheels stood outside. In his heart, too, were many thoughts, but there was no one to listen to them. Only Merry, who was supposed to be having a nap on a pile of cloaks folded across a bench far at the end of the hall, saw him. Softly she tiptoed to a table nearby and selected a few morsels of pudding, caught them up in her skirt, and with her music box tucked under one arm, stole outside.

In the brief silence, before the applause following Cornplanter's speech, Suzanne heard the faint tinkle of the music box. She looked about for Merry, and saw that she was not in the hall. She leaned out of the window in the direction from which the sound of the music box had come. Her hand fluttered to her throat. There, sitting on the ground outside the stockade, were Merry and Silverheels. Merry had taken the lid off the box and was showing Silverheels the mechanism inside. The Indian's head was bent over hers, and to Suzanne it looked as if his dark shadow engulfed her. Without stopping for her wraps she ran outside and in one sweeping, protective gesture snatched the child to her.

Silverheels did not bother to look at Suzanne. Very carefully he replaced the lid on the box and put it into Merry's hands. "Music is very pretty and happy like the little *Apetotha*." He turned away. In his bearing was the sorrowful dignity of Cornplanter, still impressed on Suzanne's mind.

Wanting somehow, suddenly, to make amends for her rudeness, she called to him, "Silverheels!" Then, not knowing what to say, she pointed to the food Merry still clutched in her skirt. "You forgot the pudding Merry brought you."

Silverheels drew himself to his full height, though his eyes were like lamps from which the light had just been snuffed. "The crumb of happiness from the white man's table has been taken from Silverheels. He will not lift his hand again."

His shoulders stiff with pride, he glided away on silver-moccasined feet.

Merry turned accusingly to Suzanne. "You sent him away! Now he won't come again!"

The full realization of what she had done swept over Suzanne. Once before, at the Point, and now again, she had cut off the only visible link with her father. Moreover, she had injured Silverheels as surely as if she had taken Winthrop's musket from the doorway of the boat cabin and fired it point-blank.

"Wait!" she called.

Silverheels quickened his stride and disappeared down snowy Sacra Via.

CHAPTER TEN

Suzanne could not sleep that night. Try as she would, she could not escape the vision of Silverheels' sorrowful eyes and his walk, stiff with pride and dignity, as he disappeared between the mounds of the ancient sacred way. She thought of Winthrop and his faith in Silverheels. What if Silverheels actually had come with word of her father? She heard again Merry's accusing voice: "You sent him away. Now he won't come again."

She slipped to the window, hoping to work the charm that had always helped when she was troubled. This time, when she opened her eyes, there was only the blank, unanswering night. The charm was, after all, only a childhood game, she told herself sadly. The realization was like the sadness of putting away a beloved doll forever. Nothing could help her but herself.

By dawn she was up and dressed. "There's no escaping the one thing I must do," she said, half aloud. "I must find Silverheels." Some relief came with the decision.

But how could she go about finding him? She could not turn to Winthrop for advice. He had gone with Anselm to Duck Creek to cut and store ice. Even if he were here, she would not have the courage to face him with the admission of her guilt. She felt that she could never face him until she had set things right by herself. Mrs. McKnight would certainly not approve of her going alone to look for Silverheels. Even if she did slip away, in what direction should she look? No matter how impossible it seemed, she nevertheless was determined to find a way to begin her search this very morning.

Mrs. McKnight unwittingly provided part of the answer at breakfast. "Word has come down the Muskingum that the youngest Shipman child is ailing with the croup," she said. "I know my oil of juniper would help. But to go afoot the distance to their cabin would be too much for me. Besides, I've set flax to soak and dare not leave it."

Suzanne forced herself to swallow a spoonful of dry mush. The Shipmans had chosen to build at once on their outlying lot near the rapids of Wolf Creek, for it was expected that the Ohio Company would be erecting a grist and saw mill there. Silverheels' lodge was this side of Shipman's! Of course, it was the place to which, lonely and sick in spirit, he would most likely turn. "I'll go, if you've no special chore planned for me today," she offered with downcast eyes. She waited for Mrs. McKnight's reply.

"Now that the treaty has been signed, you should be able to go abroad in safety," the woman said brightly. Then her voice filled with doubt. "Still, the trip might be ill-advised. I think it best that you ask General Putnam if the woods are really cleared of the savages. I hope they are. My conscience gives me no ease when I know there are sick, helpless folk about and I am powerless to help them."

"How good she is," thought Suzanne, her own conscience stirring unpleasantly. Was Mrs. McKnight only pretending not to notice her burning cheeks? With effort, Su-

118

zanne raised her eyes. The woman's back was turned; she was already rummaging in the cupboard among her small stock of herbs and tonics.

General Putnam was not so easily won over. "A journey to Shipman's?" Then his interest shifted to something outside the land office window.

Suzanne turned curiously to follow his gaze. At sight of the dusky figure grinning through the pane, she gasped with fright.

"You see?" Putnam wagged a finger in gentle banter. "The sight of a painted face even here in the stockade unnerves you!" He motioned for the man to enter. "Don't fear. It is only Peter Nyswonger dressed for his tour of duty through the woods. *Hetuck* has ordered our spies to adopt the Indian costume, for swifter movement and easier concealment."

Nyswonger bent to enter the doorway, put a hand to his shaggy black head in salute, and stood at attention. His thick legs were wrapped in deerskin, his wide shoulders bulged under his fringed jacket, and his broad, dark face was streaked with red stain. "Yes, sir?" he rumbled.

"What do the rangers report of the area this side of Wolf Creek?"

"Well cleared, sir," Nyswonger boomed. "Because the Muskingum is completely frozen, the Miamis, Wyandots, and Delawares have abandoned the canoe route by which they came. When they are through gathering their treatygifts and their belongings at their encampment back of Fort Harmar, they return to their villages by the ridge route to the north."

119

"Well, then, Suzanne," Putnam agreed with an expansive gesture, "the way is clear. If Mrs. McKnight's oil of juniper will make the Shipman child well, I see no reason why you should not make the journey. But not afoot, of course. My Toby—"

"Oh, thank you, sir! But afoot is all I know!" Suzanne's eagerness turned to dismay. "I—could never stay aboard a horse. Not even your good Toby."

Putnam rose, pondering the problem. "Can you drive?"

"Sometimes I have driven, when there were sacks of meal to deliver to Ligonier neighbors." Suzanne spoke uncertainly, trying to swallow down the lump that came in her throat with the remembering.

"Nyswonger, harness Toby to that little sleigh I had Jonathan Devol build for me, when winter first set in. It is shod with good iron runners, and Toby himself has new shoes. He's docile enough to the rein, Suzanne, and you've nothing to fear, but he may want to step out and show off, come a straight stretch on the river." He turned again to the scout. "Keep special watch over the girl as you go your rounds."

"Yes, sir!"

Suzanne stole another glance at the painted face, and saw that it was not frightening at all if one looked beyond the red streaks.

She thanked General Putnam, then hurried back to report to Mrs. McKnight and to get ready for her long, cold ride. It took only a few minutes. She kissed an unhappy Merry goodby and told her to be a good girl. She took the bundle Mrs. McKnight offered her.

"Is this all oil of juniper?" she cried.

The woman laughed. "Oh, no! There's a bit of venison here, and pudding, besides a few other things from the feast! A pity they could not have come to partake of it."

Clad in her warmest cloak and her warmest hood, Suzanne moved clumsily through the main gate. Winthrop's long leggings half covered her brogues and their flapping nearly tripped her at every step. Mrs. McKnight followed her out and down to the river bank; a buffalo robe was thrown over one arm and a heated stone wrapped in a flannel bag was hanging from the other. "Keep your hood pulled tight. I don't want you coming back with an earache."

Suzanne nodded silently and tried to quicken her pace. Peter Nyswonger already stood waiting, Toby's bridle in hand, with the little sleigh. The ranger's huge hands helped Suzanne into the sleigh. Mrs. McKnight tucked the robe securely about her, setting the heated stone slab under her feet.

"Give Mrs. Shipman my love. Be sure to tell her to measure two teaspoons of the juniper oil into a quart kettle of water. When the water steams well she is to set it under or by the child's cradle, first having covered the cradle with a tent of blankets—"

"Ready?" asked Nyswonger, handing Suzanne the reins.

The girl, white-faced, turned suddenly to Mrs. McKnight.

"You're off!" shouted Nyswonger, whacking the dappled gray soundly across the flank, and the startled horse bolted across the ice.

Mrs. McKnight moved to call Suzanne back, but kept

her silence. She stood watching until the sled disappeared around the rainbow bend. "She was afraid to go," she murmured. "I should have waited for Winthrop's return, and sent him. Yet every minute lost, with croup—" She turned on Nyswonger, who was gathering his gear and checking his weapons in readiness for his tour of duty. "If you hadn't whacked that horse, she'd be safely with me at the fireside!" She threw up her hands, despairing, then added remorsefully, "It's all my fault!"

With a final glare at the scout, she pulled her cloak collar up about her face and marched up the bank toward the main gate of Campus Martius. Nyswonger stared after her a moment, scratching his head in mute bewilderment.

After the first surprise, Toby trotted along at an even, settled pace on the river where the archway of bare trees threw a network of shadows on the snow. Then, as the sleigh neared an open stretch, he neighed shrilly, leaned into the shafts, and sent a crystal spray flying from his hoofs. Suzanne clutched the reins tightly. It was not the speed at which the horse was traveling, or the fear of being upset if the hissing runners should strike something hidden under the snow, that made her sit so rigidly. It was the old, unreasonable fear of Silverheels. It returned to her sharply now, as she recalled each encounter: the rainy night on the Ohio when the lightning had burned his face into her memory; the shock of the ice-blue stare that met hers when she had snapped the limb of the oak tree; the afternoon she had watched helpless from the top of the mound as he held his sharp knife above Merry; his dark shadow swallowing the child as he bent over her to peer inside the music box.

Only the last memory—his face as he had turned away at Campus Martius—did not chill her with fear.

She must get hold of herself, she reasoned, and tugged on Toby's reins until the horse slowed to a plodding, head-bobbing walk. She recalled each scene one by one and pointed out to herself how mistaken her fear and mistrust of Silverheels had been. The very night she had drawn back in terror at the sight of the half-breed in the lightning, he had saved her father. From the tree at the Point, Silverheels had returned to his lodge to care for him. He had left his lodge at her father's request and come into the settlement to tell them of Josiah's safety. When it had appeared Silverheels was menacing Merry, he had instead cut a coin from his moccasin that she might have a plaything. When his dark shadow had seemed to consume her, he was only sharing with her a childlike delight in the music box. All she had to fear from Silverheels, Suzanne told herself, was that he would not forgive her distrust of him.

The frosty air, the clean, pure light, sharpened her senses to a keen pitch. In this world about her where even the shadows were clearly defined, it did not seem possible that her father could have disappeared and left no trace. Somewhere there must be a clue. Carefully she lined up the pitifully few facts that had led up to nothing. Silverheels had said the Delawares captured her father and took him from the hut. St. Clair's spies reported a white man traveling with a Delaware hunting party along the Great Miami. But the Delaware chief, Captain Pipes, insisted the white man was a British trader, not a captive. A sudden thought struck her more deeply and surely than anything the charm

One after another the familiar. landmarks slipped past

had ever worked. Yes, it was possible. For reasons of his own Captain Pipes might not be telling the truth. The white man might be her father! She flipped the reins over Toby's back until the speed of the sleigh again matched her flying thoughts.

One after another the familiar landmarks slipped past and merged into the white distance behind her. Twice she caught sight of Peter Nyswonger, mounted on a large roan, among the tree trunks. He seemed to be signalling her to slow her pace. Then Mrs. McKnight's neatly tied parcel jolted sharply against her side as if to remind her of her errand. She braced her feet against the high dashboard and tugged at the reins until Toby settled into an easy jog. She resigned herself at first to watching for Shipman's cabin, above the western bank of the river, but after a while her gaze strayed often to the eastern shore. Silverheels' lodge, Winthrop had told her, was half concealed in the brush above a riffle a short way from a creek mouth on that side.

Rounding the bend, she caught her breath sharply as she saw tracks of an unshod horse leading from a ravine onto the river bed. She followed them where they skirted the shoreline under the great white arms of the sycamores, cut across a rock-bordered cove, around another bend, past a frozen riffle, and on to the mouth of a small creek. There they ended. In the shelter of the bank a rough-coated horse nuzzled grain freshly spread on the snow. Moccasin tracks led upward over the slope and disappeared into a thicket. Fearfully, hopefully, her eyes probed through the bare branches for a glimpse of a pole hut, traced its outlines, and saw the solid patch of snow-covered roof.

Suzanne stood up in the sleigh. "Hello-o!" she called shakily. When there was no answer she called again, more loudly. *"Silverheels!"* She listened intently but heard only the wind in the trees. Shaken, she sat down again, wondering what to do next. Then she noticed that the moccasin tracks led down as well as up. Her eyes leaped to a dark figure almost a quarter of a mile ahead on the ice. She flipped the reins over Toby's back. There would be no stopping now.

She cut straight for the figure. As she drew nearer there was no doubt that it was Silverheels. He crouched, spear poised, over a hole in the ice. Suzanne drew up sharply. Silverheels did not glance her way. He straightened slowly, fish gig in hand, and stood rigid, not once taking his eyes from the dark water surging under the ice. Suddenly he thrust viciously downward. The spear shaft quivered with an invisible struggle. With a quick jerk he lifted the spear, swung it over the ice, shook off a large pike, and flung it into a wriggling sack.

Suzanne's stomach wriggled and flopped like the fish-filled bag, but she managed to speak as politely as if she were at a social gathering at Campus Martius. "They're very good this time of year."

Silverheels appeared to notice her for the first time. "You tire out horse to tell Silverheels the *amatha* he spear are good?"

Suzanne shrank deeper into the buffalo robe, but her eyes did not falter before the chill gaze. "No," she blurted, "I came to tell you I'm sorry."

Silverheels stared at her for a moment, then turned his

back and crouched again over the hole in the ice. "Girl with eyes like *miskeque,* the pond, say she is sorry. For what?"

"For acting as if you were not my friend."

"The little firehead is Silverheels' *necana,* his friend. She does not look at him as at an evil spirit. You?" He shrugged his shoulders expressively.

Suzanne bit her lip to keep back the tears. "My brother is your friend. He believes in your vow to find my father—"

Silverheels lifted a hand for silence. "Silverheels has gone far on the old ways of the ridges, the valley, and the waters in search of the brave little man. Nowhere has he found him. Is enough. Silverheels punish some other way enemies who stole sick man from his lodge while yet under Silverheels' *midewiwin.*"

Suzanne wet her stiff lips. "Silverheels!"

Something in her voice made him turn, his fish gig still poised.

"Governor St. Clair's agents told of a white man in a Delaware hunting camp. Monsieur La Chapelle questioned the Delaware chief at Harmar. Captain Pipes said the man was a British trader, not a captive." She paused. "Maybe the Delaware chief was not telling the truth!"

Silverheels' eyes glinted. "No Delaware tell truth!" His hand moved slowly along the length of his spear. "Winter hunting camps change with the wind, but Silverheels' feet are swift."

Suzanne threw aside the robe and stepped awkwardly from the sleigh. "Then you'll help us again? This camp was reported along the Great Miami. But you'll go?"

He nodded, and the chill of his eyes thawed. He spoke

swiftly in the voice soft from living so much alone. "The shy one is brave after all, like her father. Though small, much spirit. Silverheels offer hand of friendship." His large cold hand clasped hers briefly. "You go now. Ranger man who play Indian coming through brush. Silverheels does not like spies."

Suzanne saw no trace of Peter Nyswonger, but obeyed Silverheels and with one backward glance of gratitude, turned to the sleigh.

"Campus Martius other way!" Silverheels called.

"I'm taking some medicine to Shipman's," she explained.

"Is only the distance the sun casts its shadow from the hill." He raised his arm in salute.

Suzanne turned into the wind, her head and heart light with joy. Silverheels was her friend. The broken link to her father had been welded. The runners seemed to echo over the snow and ice, "Only the distance the sun casts its shadow from the hill."

Never had her father seemed so near.

CHAPTER ELEVEN

Judge Varnum's death, so long expected, came almost simultaneously with the completion of the treaty. His funeral, held with much solemnity and ceremony, was attended not only by the officials and the populace, but also by the Indians still lingering in the area.

Chief Cornplanter and his party did not, in fact, move northward until the twentieth of January. A few days later, after approving plans for surveying Donation Tracts for outsettlements on Wolf Creek and Duck Creek, and down the Ohio River at a spot opposite the mouth of the Little Kanawha River, Governor St. Clair and others set off upriver to take care of business matters, both private and public, in the East. The Ohio Company directors appointed a committee to inspect the best locations for mill seats.

The work of the mill committee was unhappily delayed. A sudden thaw in the ice-bound Ohio and Muskingum Rivers brought a jamming of ice floes and a flooding of the Point such as the settlers had never expected, though General Putnam had warned them of the likelihood before they built their cabins and storehouses there.

Even as they were drying out around the stockade at the Point, plans were going forward for a great ball to be held on Thursday, the fifth of February, at Campus Martius. The wedding of Colonel Winthrop Sargent—Secretary of the Territory North West of the River Ohio and, during the absence of the Governor, the superintendent of its affairs —and pretty Rowena Tupper, a sister of Anselm, was to take place on Friday, the sixth. The ceremony would be performed by the bride's father, Judge Benjamin Tupper, since Parson Story, the preacher promised them by the Ohio Company, had not yet arrived to take up his duties.

Suzanne and Merry chattered excitedly over what they heard concerning the wedding plans; they hoped to catch a glimpse of the festivities. Winthrop Lake's mind went only as far as Monday, the second day of February, at nine o'clock in the forenoon, the time mentioned, in the writ for his arrest and summons, for his appearance before the Court of Common Pleas.

Early on that morning, having nothing else to do, he followed Anselm down the river bank to the wharf at the Point to inspect the damage the high water had done. It was a bleak scene with many big cakes of ice still riding the waves lashed up by a raw north wind.

"Cheer up!" Anselm clapped him on the shoulder. "By your long face you'd think you had to appear before the Grand Jury instead of before the County Court of Common Pleas—presided over by my father!"

Winthrop glanced over his shoulder in the direction of the jail, a stout log cabin on the plain just outside the stockade of the Picketed Point. "How many days could I be sentenced for, for disturbing the peace?"

Anselm laughed. "Haven't I told you time and again that you weren't disturbing the peace when you collared

130

that trader? You were maintaining the peace won by the treaty. That's your defense."

Winthrop's mouth went dry. "I'm not good at speech-making."

"Maybe you won't have to be. I think Colonel Sproat just wanted someone to practice on, when he served you notice."

Winthrop nodded, swallowing hard. "Well, I'll be glad when it's over."

Anselm squinted at the watery sun. "Court sits in about an hour. Perhaps we'd better be getting back that way, before we're late and you're charged with contempt of court! And—" He broke off and stood gazing across the choppy river toward the island midstream.

Winthrop looked to see what had drawn Anselm's attention. Passing the island tip was a Kentucky boat. It seemed to be drifting aimlessly with the wind and current and ice.

"Don't see anybody on deck," Anselm murmured. "Do you suppose it broke loose from somewhere upstream?" He cupped his hands and shouted: "Ho, there! Anyone aboard?"

A boatman's horn answered feebly and the craft swung slowly about. As the distance between it and the wharf narrowed, Winthrop made out a muffled figure bending to the sweep. "A female!" he exclaimed. "I guess she's trying to bring it to dock."

"Bear to your right!" Anselm shouted across the water. "More! Now cast your line!"

A small boy came from the cabin, uncoiled the mooring rope and flung it futilely toward shore. Anselm said something under his breath, kicked off his boots, swam the gap of white-capped, ice-troubled river, and returned with the rope in his teeth. Winthrop drew Anselm from the water, shivering and gasping with the cold. Together they shouldered the rope and tugged until the boat nudged against the wharf.

"Land o' mercy," quavered the gray-faced woman bundled in a grayish cloak, still clutching the sweep, but now leaning on it for support. "There was nary a soul on the river to help us."

"We need help bad," the child said between blue lips.

"Make fast the line," Anselm directed Winthrop and dropped into the bow. He boosted the boy to the wharf and turned to the woman. "If you need help you've come to the right place."

The frail middle-aged woman looked up gallantly from under the heavy scarf tied about her chin. "It's not me that needs help. It's the mister. He's took sick."

"We ain't et for two days," piped the boy.

Winthrop and Anselm exchanged glances.

"Where is the master?" Anselm asked.

"In the cabin. Reckon it'll take both of you strangers to get him out and ashore. Mr. Welsh is not a big man, but he's mighty weak and some touched with fever. I've heard tell a man by name of Moses Morse has rooms to rent to travelers. If your kind selves would lead us there—" She gathered her skirts about her and, declining Anselm's arm, stepped unaided onto the wharf.

132

"Mr. Welsh?" Anselm called into the shadows.

"Come in!" A thin, slightly rasping voice answered. "I ain't got the plague. Jest another touch of the fever picked up in the army."

"The madam says you want to come ashore." Anselm stepped across the threshold.

"Sure could tolerate to rest with ye folks a spell afore goin' on to Kaintuck. My woman can do nigh anything but pilot a boat." He attempted to rise from the bunk in a dim corner and fell back weakly.

Anselm and Winthrop hurried to the bunkside. The man looked thin and wasted, wrapped though he was in a padded patchwork quilt. His beard was unkempt, but his hair was tied neatly back. "Is the Morse tavern for likes of us?" he asked, rising on one elbow. "I've only a few shillings put by, but in the cargo there's hog lard—"

"Steady, now," Anselm said. "Hold to our shoulders and we'll have you ashore and comfortable in no time. Yonder is Morse's Row." He nodded toward the four long boxlike houses lining the bank.

"No, not one room left," Moses Morse stated flatly, his narrow eyes shifting from the quilted figure to Anselm; and hastily he bolted fast the door.

"We ain't et for two days!" The small boy whimpered.

The woman's face sagged wearily. "We've come this far, hoping—"

"There are good folk here who'll welcome you as neighbors," Anselm softly interrupted. "Come along."

"To Mrs. Owen's?" Winthrop asked, as they turned toward her door.

"Where else? Where else would they have better care—unless it's at Widow McKnight's, and that's too far to take him. Since Judge Varnum is gone, and she has no one else to be nurse to, she'll have the room, and the time, and the good heart she'll need."

Winthrop nodded, understanding, and the group continued its halting way under the gray sky toward Mrs. Owen's doorstep.

At Winthrop's knock, the woman opened the door a crack, then threw it wide open. "Bless my soul! What have we here? Trouble?"

As Winthrop stepped aside, Anselm helped Mr. Welsh forward. Mrs. Welsh peered nervously from behind Anselm's shoulder and the small boy stood silently shivering, holding to a corner of the quilt.

"This is Mr. Welsh and family," Anselm said lamely.

"From the headwaters of the Youghiogheny," the woman said, "and the mister has took sick, but we don't aim to trouble nobody," she added, with stiff dignity.

"We ain't et for two days," the small boy persisted.

"Hush your mouth," his mother chided gently.

"I thought you might give Mr. Welsh a tonic and let the woman and child warm themselves—" Anselm began.

"Of course!" Mrs. Owen gasped, with her hands to her cheeks. "And here I stand! I was just so taken by surprise," she apologized. She extended a welcoming hand to Mrs. Welsh. "We don't have many visitors this time of year. Just sit by the fire and I'll start some tea and get out a bit of johnnycake for the little lad, to hold him until I can mix hot gruel. You young men, now! Lay Mr. Welsh on the bed

in the back room. Then run right along." She pointed to
Anselm's still dripping clothing and Winthrop's muddy
boots. "You get home and get dry before you come down
with the ague, or worse, Anselm. And you, Master Lake, if
you're appearing in court this morning, as summoned, better
scrape the mud from your boots first. I'll take care of things
here."

Grateful to be thus dismissed, they hurried out. For
Winthrop, there was not much time to lose. As they hastened toward Campus Martius, Anselm insisted that wet
clothes or not, he was going to attend the court. Suddenly
he interrupted himself with a big sneeze.

"See? Better do as Mrs. Owen advised!" Winthrop told
him with a laugh. "Go dry out."

"And miss the sight of your face when *Hetuck* reads the
charge laid against you?"

"Yes." Winthrop's attempt at a smile was weak. "I'd
rather be condemned without too many friendly onlookers."

They parted by the main gate. Winthrop squared his
shoulders and walked on alone to the northwest blockhouse.

A guard of the militia stood at attention by the closed
doorway of the hall. Though Winthrop had drilled beside
him on the parade ground, the soldier gave no sign of
recognition. Stiffly he opened the door. Winthrop hesitated
on the threshold. His glance shied from the sprinkling of
citizens from the Point and Campus Martius who sat on the
rear benches. The front row was separated from the assembly
by a wide gap of empty benches. Winthrop decided he be-
longed there and, cheeks burning, sat down on the hard bench.

Strange how the same place could look different, ac-

Winthrop hesitated on the threshold

cording to what use it was being put to, he reflected. After the treaty-signing, this hall had been a place of feasting, full of fragrant warmth, fellowship, and good cheer. When the women gathered to spin, it hummed with industry. Judge Varnum's funeral had given it lofty solemnity and pomp. On the Sabbath, when Dr. Solomon Drowne or Colonel Ebenezer Battelle conducted religious service, it was a place of quiet peace. If the stockaded dwellings should be attacked, these same four walls would serve as refuge for the women and children. Now, though the judges had not yet made their entrance, the hall had the air of a courtroom.

Winthrop stared fixedly at the doorway when he heard the tread of feet along the corridor outside. The guard flung the door open and the people in the hall rose as one person. Colonel Ebenezer Sproat, carrying the staff of High Sheriff, entered, followed by three magistrates and a clerk. Though the judges wore no official robes, they were cloaked in dignity. The pallid clerk, who kept accounts for Captain Prince, the hatter at the Point, had assumed added stature.

The judges lined themselves in solid rank behind the table; the clerk took his place beside a small lectern and opened a black ledger. Colonel Sproat's fierce dark eyes swept the room until there was complete silence. Then he tapped the floor with his staff of office and began in a deep voice, "Hear ye! Hear ye! Court is opened for the administration of even-handed justice to the poor and the rich, to the guilty and the innocent. Please be seated."

Colonel Sproat remained standing. He tucked a thumb inside his vest and considered the notes half concealed in one large hand. "Winthrop Lake!" he sang out.

Winthrop rose quickly and went forward. Colonel Sproat turned to the judges. "Winthrop Lake is charged with disturbing the peace," he read for all to hear. "On the day of brotherhood, when all were bending every effort toward peace and harmony in celebration of the Fort Harmar Treaty, he attacked, without warning, a trader come into our midst bent on pursuing his honorable profession." He swung toward Winthrop. "Does the defendant admit the charge?"

"Not exactly, sir," Winthrop said, looking down.

"What has the accused to say in defense of himself?"

"Nothing, sir." Winthrop did not lift his eyes.

Hetuck's big face grew uneasy and his voice lowered to an almost courteous tone. "If the accused will not speak in his own defense, mayhap he has a witness who will stand for him?"

"None, sir," Winthrop said doggedly, still not lifting his eyes.

There was a stir in the back of the hall. Suzanne rose, her blue eyes bright under her sprigged velvet bonnet, her white face set with pride and a hint of disdain. "I stand for him." She lifted her skirts gracefully above the tip of her stout brogues and came forward.

Colonel Sproat, taken by surprise, forgot formalities. The girl put him in mind, for a moment, of his own Sally back in Massachusetts waiting for him to come and bring her to the Ohio Country. "Be heard, Mistress Lake."

Suzanne's gaze went past him to the judges. Her words tumbled out as if she knew she must have her say quickly or she would turn and flee. "Winthrop has been taught by a good father that all men are to be honored, that a foe bested in any way is not to be despised. The trader was insulting the Indians invited to the feast—" she hesitated, then went on— "in language no lady should hear. Winthrop stepped in to defend the feelings of both. For this he is arrested! And what did the women do?" she added, her mounting indignation overcoming her shyness. "They ran after the trader clamoring for salt for their boiling pots! Without a word of thanks."

138

The first judge pulled his lean jaw, the second drew a kerchief from his sleeve and dabbed at his mouth, the third —Judge Benjamin Tupper himself—took off his square-rimmed spectacles and wiped them vigorously. They leaned their heads together, mumbled briefly, and turned to the clerk. The clerk's quill scratched across a parchment. He handed it to the red-faced Colonel Sproat.

"Not guilty!" Sproat boomed, looking immensely relieved. "Case dismissed."

Winthrop, in order to make his haste less apparent, bowed slightly toward the dignitaries. Then, with a glance of pride and astonishment at Suzanne, he led her outside.

"I—don't know how to thank you, Susu, for knowing what to say. And saying it. You told more about why I did what I did than I knew myself! I'll let you run and break the news to Mrs. McKnight and Merry." He was starting for the main gate.

"But aren't you coming to break the news to them yourself?"

He paused. "I was thinking I'd better go see how the boat is, since the thaw and all."

Suzanne nodded and did not press him further. She knew he had many things he wanted to think over, now that the dread of a possible jail sentence had been lifted from him. And he could do his best thinking there on the boat that was a part of home.

Winthrop did not know how long he stayed there, puttering about the boat. Riding high it was now, without its cargo of meal. His heart was higher and lighter than it had been, too. It suddenly came to him that he felt a little lighter in the stomach than ordinarily, also. He was hungry. There had been little appetite for his early breakfast. By now it must be mid-afternoon.

He had just clambered out of the boat and was on his way up the slope when he heard Anselm hail him. Anselm was coming to meet him. Winthrop noted with surprise the sharp lines of anxiety on his friend's face. Perhaps he hadn't heard. Perhaps he was expecting a guard to approach any moment to lead him off to a jail sentence! If that was so, Winthrop would have a little fun with him.

Putting on a gloomy face, he hurried forward. "Perhaps I could beg from you the loan of three pounds, ten shillings, for fine and costs?" he began.

"Glad to help," Anselm said absently, reaching into his pocket.

Winthrop's surprise heightened. One did not advance such a sum as if it were a bag of shells. He dropped his pretense when Anselm's expression did not clear. "What's the matter? You look as if you'd seen a ghost."

"Worse," Anselm muttered. "I've been at Mr. Welsh's bedside. Dr. Farley was there, too." Anselm drew a deep, shuddering breath. "He fears—he is almost certain—that Mr. Welsh is the victim of smallpox."

Winthrop stared for a startled second, reading in Anselm's haggard face the stark dread of epidemic, and the knowledge that the disease had been in the very air they breathed that morning. "I've done a terrible thing," Anselm said. "When I brought Mr. Welsh into the stockade at Picketed Point, I brought in Death."

"But you weren't alone in it," Winthrop reminded him.

He looked down at his own hands and slowly wiped them on his breeches.

"I should not have been so careless. I was in the army long enough, saw devastation enough from what seemed at first to be a simple fever—yet it never even occurred to me that I might be taking a chance. Now you have been ex-posed—"

"Do not worry about me," Winthrop shrugged that off. "What about Mrs. Owen?"

"For herself, she fears nothing. She says the people may remain; she will care for them. And unless he is sure, Dr. Farley does not want to run the chance of spoiling the week's festivities by sounding a false alarm. However, if his diagnosis proves accurate, he is determined that a meeting of all the citizens shall be called, the situation presented to them, and a mass inoculation recommended."

Winthrop nodded. "In the meantime, you and I—?"

"Be on the alert. Be prepared for anything." The two separated, solemnly and in silence.

The following week, a town meeting was called and assembled in the big hall. General Putnam called the citizens to order. Dr. Thomas Farley rose from behind the table to address them. He was a small-boned man with silver-spec-tacled blue eyes that gazed unflinchingly over the crowd.

"No need to dwell on the horrors of the smallpox epi-demic that threatens our settlement," he began crisply. "I propose a mass experiment to check it." With a precise snap he unlatched the black bag on the table, took out a shining knife, a needle, a small bottle, and laid them on a bleached

Dr. Farley laid his implements on a bleached cloth

cloth. "When the pox of the unfortunate man in our midst erupt, I shall draw the venom from them. Then I shall make a small cut on the arm of every man, woman, and child—all of you who have not had the disease. Into that cut I shall touch the point of a needle on which there will be a small bit of the infection. It will cause only a mild soreness and swelling of the portion treated and will prevent the disease from attacking the entire body and running its natural course of disfigurement or death."

A ripple of surprise and antagonism went through the crowd. "The doctor's mad!" the fishmonger burst out.

"It's all one to him," the blacksmith agreed. "What's a corpse one way or the other as long as he can try out his devil's gamble on us?"

"I say stow the pest-ridden man on the boat he came on and set him on his way," a hoarse voice cried.

"Silence!" Putnam roared, banging the table with his gavel. "Let us proceed with dignity. Dr. Jabez True asks for the floor."

The angry murmuring faded away and all faces turned trustfully to the tall slender figure in the old-fashioned breeches, silver-buckled shoes, and black-ribboned cue. Dr. True's patience, charity, and sympathy had at one time or another touched everyone in the colony. His one good eye looked with gentle forgiveness over the room. "Friends, have we forgotten the resolve set forth by our company of associates to pay as much attention as possible to the public welfare? Nay, let it not be so. And let it not be that our brother, dedicated to fight for a life to the end, be denied. Many of you know Dr. Farley from his practicing days in Salem. All of you know his services here. While I am of an older school and am not learned in the more advance medicine, I say I have heard of the success of the experiment in the army. He has my complete trust. I suggest that not only shall we undergo the treatment, but also that we build small wards on the plain by the mound Conus, away from all else, where the experiment may be conducted." He switched his long cue back and forth and sat down.

The proprietors of the small shops along Merchants'

Row at the Point began to whisper among themselves. To expose the entire settlement willfully to the disease because of the illness of one man who happened to be passing by was folly, said one. Another spoke up and reminded them that the place would be branded and passersby would avoid landing there for months even for supplies. Business would come to a standstill.

"How many months have your trades and businesses been protected by our rangers, by the militia, and by the guns of Campus Martius?" shouted Colonel Sproat. "Now, when one of the associates proposes something for the common good you think only of your money pots."

Noticing the trend toward division of opinion between Campus Martius and the Point, John Matthews spoke. "Whether our homes are at the Point or at Campus Martius, we are citizens together in the township of Marietta," he said. "Let us proceed with that in mind."

"Who is there among us to dispute the wisdom of Dr. True and Dr. Farley?" a mild voice challenged. "I say, let us submit. But first, before building our own pest huts, it seems to me the ailing man should be provided with one at once so that he may be removed from our midst."

Anselm, with a set face, rose from the crowd. "I ask that if such a hut is built, I may build it. It is my request also that I may conduct the victim thither."

"Why not?" An accusing voice came from the back of the hall. "It was your folly, Anselm Tupper, that brought the smallpox among us."

Anselm turned around to search out the speaker, his eyes glinting dangerously. No one moved.

144

General Putnam sensibly took over the silence by calling for a vote. "The hut for Mr. Welsh shall be built on the plain," he announced presently. "Unless there is further outbreak of the smallpox, Dr. Farley's experiment will not be used. Let us all go straight to our homes and pay the strictest attention to our own duties, mingling with one another only when necessity demands."

Within the hour, Anselm went to the uplands to hew logs. By morning the small hut, looking to his gloomy eye like an oversize coffin, stood alone on the plain. Then he drove an ox-cart to the Point and up to Mrs. Owen's door. There was no one in sight to protest, but Anselm could feel the gaze of many eyes from behind drawn shutters.

Mrs. Owen helped him carry the sick man outside and load him into the cart. "Drive over the stumps as careful as you can," she directed, "and cover him from the air." With a penetrating look at Anselm, she added, "Your shoulders are stout, young man, but no one was meant to take to himself the burden you're carrying."

Anselm stared at her mutely, attempted a wan smile, took the ox by one horn and, walking slowly, led the creaking cart away.

Mr. Welsh lived only a few days after he was moved to the hut on the plain. The month of February crept to a wretched end. Under curtains of rain and dismal fog, the settlement looked abandoned.

Word of the first death, then the next, then the next traveled from wall to wall at Merchants' Row at the Point, through the woods to Campus Martius, and across the Muskingum to Fort Harmar. A meeting was called again, and those who ventured out this time approved Dr. Farley's plan for mass inoculation. A row of huts was built, back of the lone one in which Mr. Welsh had died, and there, sleeves rolled up in spite of the cold, Anselm went from bunkside to bunkside, helping Dr. True and Dr. Farley.

General Putnam tried to busy himself with papers at the land office, but kept looking out the window toward the plain and wondering when there would no longer be treaties, famine, or epidemics; when the fortifications—the pickets and the abatis of forked tree trunks—could be removed from the dwellings and the colony would become the City of Brothers, *Adelphi,* that he had visualized and that Judge Varnum and others had originally chosen to name it.

Winthrop lay in the tiny pest house he had built for himself. He watched the throbbing swelling on his arm and was thankful that he was taking the disease by inoculation instead of in the "natural" way. Even so, the walls of the hut seemed to be swinging in a mist. When Dr. Farley bent in the doorway to tend him, Winthrop mumbled feverishly, "Father?"

His sisters were only touched by discomfort for a day or two, while Mrs. McKnight grimly battled a mild case of the disease, but refused to be away from her duties and household long.

In Mrs. McKnight's kitchen, Suzanne listened while Merry played the music box, and kept an anxious eye on the bread baking on the hearth. As she leaned closer, she impatiently pinned her braids high in a crown around her head to keep them from the ashes. Then she lifted the fragrant loaf, wrapped it with trembling fingers in a clean cloth and, with a quick pat on Merry's curls, snatched her cape from the peg and hurried bareheaded outside. She walked swiftly down the woodland path and through the cornfields rustling with last year's dried stalks until she came to the edge of the plain where the pest houses huddled forlornly.

When she saw Anselm striding up the river road, a yoke of leather water buckets across his shoulder, she tried to call but no sound came. When he saw her he paused, set the yoke aside, and came over to her. His nose twitched appreciatively at the scent of the bread she held clutched close to her with both hands. "For Winthrop to sup on?" he inquired.

"It is for you, Anselm," she replied, shyly holding toward him the loaf still warm in its cloth wrapping.

Anselm took it questioningly. "For me?"

"You've not been resting, or taking time to eat, so I thought—" Suzanne stammered, unable to go on.

Anselm bent and peered into her flushed face under the pale gold crown of braids. "Sometimes you're not like a child at all. Not at all. This is your way of taking up for me, as they say you did for Winthrop at his trial, isn't it?" He moved a step closer.

Without a word, Suzanne spun and fled, her heart beating with a flurry of strange emotions.

Anselm watched the girl's slight figure running through the cornstalks until her fluttering cape was out of sight. For the first time in many days a smile broke over his face. Slowly, he began to hum:

> Arise my true love
> And present me your hand—

CHAPTER TWELVE

Suzanne hurried along the path through the communal gardens below Campus Martius, taking no notice of the tender green shoots of beans and squash pushing toward the April sun. Head high, cheeks burning, she made straight for their boat still moored at the wharf. Once on board she leaned against the cabin. The familiar planks were solid, reassuring, something of home. Slowly she took off her brogues, went to the bow, and lowered her feet into the cool Muskingum. She did not turn her gaze from the misty green heights across the river when she recognized Winthrop's step along the gangplank.

He sat beside her and tossed a pebble toward the willows that turned in the wind like a school of minnows showing their silver sides. "Wool-gathering?"

She shook her head mutely.

Winthrop studied her narrowly. Her face had thinned during the lean winter, but it had firmed, too, though now it looked as if at the slightest touch its rigid composure would break. "What's the matter?" he asked carefully.

She turned to him. "Winthrop, we can't go on living at Campus Martius much longer."

"Who says so?" he frowned.

"Nobody, yet."

"Well, then," he sighed with relief, "why fret?"

Suzanne's fingers nervously traced a crack in the deck. "I found out this morning that Mrs. McKnight hasn't become a shareholder. She's only keeping the rooms at Campus Martius until the real owner arrives. General Putnam arranged it so she could."

Winthrop rose in astonishment. "Why didn't she tell us sooner? Why—"

"She hasn't told us at all," Suzanne interrupted. "I just now overheard it from some women talking at the well."

"When's the real owner coming to turn her out? Who is he?" Winthrop scowled belligerently.

"I don't know. But he is someone who really intends to settle. That's why it's taken him so long to close out his affairs in the East. Oh, what are we going to do? We can't leave; we promised Father we'd wait. And what's going to happen to Mrs. McKnight? The women are wondering."

Winthrop began to walk up and down the deck. "We'll think of something." For the first time he fully understood the burden that Mrs. McKnight's anxious mothering of Suzanne and Merry had lifted from him. That she herself might need help had never occurred to him.

"We could all move onto the boat," Suzanne suggested dubiously.

Winthrop paused to consider. He'd been able to make out all right on board during the mild months, generally bunking during severe weather with Anselm, or sleeping on a pallet by the fire at Mrs. McKnight's. Now he looked more critically at the boat. The bottom had sprung several small leaks that he was trying to keep caulked up, the deck was warping, and the cabin would serve for shade but for

149

little else. Certainly it was no place for three females. They'd be living like squatters, only a frayed rope hitched to a rotting stump to moor them to land. Even with the rope replaced and repairs made— "No, it won't do," he said flatly. Once more he paced the deck. Absently he began to hum:

> The seed is blown before the wind
> And where it comes to rest
> Be it on mountain meadow green—

Suddenly he stood sentry-still as the memory of the green meadow saddling the hills swept over him. "Suzanne," he said slowly, "we may have the answer."

"What?" She looked up hopefully.

"The donation lands."

"The donation lands?" Suzanne echoed, half between laughter and anger. "This is no time to jest."

"Listen to me," Winthrop said flatly, "the land is free for the asking. I can put in for a hundred-acre share, the same as anybody else."

"It's to be given only to residents," Suzanne protested.

"So?" Winthrop's dark eyebrows lifted. "We've lived in the colony longer than most shareholders! My name on the payroll for the surveyors and the muster for the militia will prove that."

"But the person who puts in for a plot has to be a man."

"I don't know what you think makes a man," Winthrop said stiffly. "I've stood trial at a court of law, remember. As soon as I'm seventeen years old, I'll be in my eighteenth year. And I'll be head of the household, if Mrs. McKnight is no longer with us."

Suzanne's blue eyes begged forgiveness, but her tone was unyielding. "The donation lands are for people who plan to settle here. We're going on to Kentucky—" her voice faltered— "as soon as Father comes."

"Sure!" Winthrop turned his face to hide from her how little hope he held that Josiah was still alive. "But then we could deed the land with its improvements over to Mrs. McKnight," he added with a side glance at Suzanne.

"Mrs. McKnight always has said that this is the only land worth settling," Suzanne said thoughtfully. "She's seen a good deal of the country."

Winthrop impetuously caught up Suzanne's hand. "Come on, there's a place I want you to see! There's no harm looking."

Mrs. McKnight put down her mending and glanced suspiciously from one to the other. "And what reason have you two to go roaming up that way? The section is, I believe, part of the Donation Tract."

"It's an uncommonly pretty site for an outing," Winthrop answered airily.

Mrs. McKnight compressed her lips. "Has Anselm Tupper or anyone else been putting notions into your head?"

"Only that the land is free to the homeless for the settling and the keeping of it." Winthrop watched her shrewdly.

The woman's head bent to her mending. "I fail to see that it is of any concern to us. Well?" She looked up sharply "Who here is homeless?"

Winthrop shuffled his feet and Suzanne gulped.

151

Mrs. McKnight rose abruptly. "I don't know why you two are looking so guilty. La! If you're of a mind to have a lark, why not? It's been a hard winter." She went to the back room and in a few minutes returned with a basket. "Since the boat with supplies passed yesterday there's bacon to spare." She handed the basket to Suzanne. "See that you return it with greens and sassafrass. An empty basket is a reproach to the idle."

She stood in the doorway looking through the main gate to the landing-place below the gardens while Winthrop helped Suzanne into the canoe, and with her gaze she followed them upriver until they were out of sight.

Winthrop's deep strokes guided the canoe smoothly through the quiet waters along the willow-fringed bank. The stir of the waking forest was all about. But Suzanne was aware of it only as one is to a melody heard from a distance, puzzled as she was by Winthrop's talk of the free lands. Of course she had heard of the Donation Tracts before, from snatches of conversation in the hall where the women sat at their spinning, or between Anselm and Winthrop as they rested on the doorstep after a surveying trip. Now it was necessary to know more.

"It's simple enough," Winthrop explained. "Thousands of families have passed down the Ohio. Many of them would have located here if they'd had a way of getting hold of land. The colony needs some of these people. It needs them for the building of mills, for strengthening its position. So, the company has chosen sites out of its holdings to grant in one-hundred-acre parcels to useful parties."

Suzanne, impressed by her brother's knowledge of affairs, sat a while in thoughtful silence. "These donation sites," she ventured, "aren't they land nobody in the company wants?"

"Land nobody wants?" Winthrop missed a stroke. "You should see the black soil along the Ohio between the Little Hocking and the bottomlands opposite the mouth of the Little Kanawha. I reckon it could yield twice the wheat and corn harvested to an acre in Ligonier Valley."

"Is the site west of the Muskingum on Wolf Creek good for farming, too?"

Winthrop made a sweeping gesture. "It's fine for farming but better for milling. The falls at the bend need only to be harnessed."

"It sounds too good to be true," Suzanne murmured. "So much for nothing."

"The New Englanders don't value everything in currency." Winthrop shrugged. "Like, for instance, security. The Donation Tracts are really outposts. Its people are bound to military law and must keep defenses approved by the company."

"I see." Suzanne nodded. "But since the treaty has been signed, there shouldn't be much risk. What else must a donation settler promise?"

"To build a dwelling at least eighteen by twenty-four feet, clear and put into pasture fifteen acres, and into tillage not less than five acres—"

Suzanne gazed in astonishment at her brother. "That kind of work takes years!"

"There's a five-year term to do it in. By that time the

settler should have planted fifty apple and twenty peach trees, and should have returned a stretch from his grant for highways."

"You mean it takes five years—all that work, those trees, before a clear title is given?"

Winthrop nodded curtly. "I'm not afraid of work."

"Neither am I," Suzanne retorted. "But Father's aim is Kentucky. We can't—"

Winthrop set his jaw stubbornly. "At least we can look," he interrupted.

Suzanne stared straight ahead. What she saw, what Winthrop must be made to see, called for another kind of sight. She gave herself up for the time being to the spell of the Muskingum.

Winthrop beached on the sandbar at the mouth of a small creek. "We'll go on afoot," he said briskly.

Suzanne looked into the shadowed forest where the creek twisted into the distance and was lost. "It's so still," she whispered, moving closer to Winthrop.

"I used to think the woods were scary, too," Winthrop admitted, taking her hand and pulling her up the creek bank to its grassy rim. "Surveying changed my way of looking at it. When you level a transit and run lines that cut out the land into neat squares of ranges, sections, and townships, you've already got it tamed."

"I thought you bounded properties by rivers, ridges, creeks, and certain trees as landmarks."

"That was in the old days, and in some areas like unexplored parts of Old Virginia, they still do. But with Thomas Hutchins as Geographer of the United States and by terms of the Ordinance of 1787 and the Ohio Company's Purchase, you don't. Suppose you and I owned this plot and our north corner boundary was that beech tree yonder. Say lightning hit the tree. How could we prove in a few years that our land extended to there?"

"I guess we couldn't."

"Oh, yes, we could!" Winthrop pushed back the brush with his boot-toe and pointed to a stake driven into a cone of earth. "See? This is a benchmark. The surveyors have been here. Even if this mark should be destroyed, the government has a record of it and can set another in its place."

Suzanne looked about her with new interest. "It does make the woods seem more civilized," she admitted. "And it helps one understand a little, too, of how the Indians feel, about having the surveyors move farther and farther into their lands."

Winthrop ignored that. "In five years there'll be a neighbor on each one-hundred-acre plot," he reminded her.

As they threaded their way upcreek, Winthrop lapsed into silence. What if the meadow was not as he remembered it, if it should turn out to be, after all, only a patch of green high in an alien wilderness? His heart beat faster the nearer they came. When the trees about them began to drip mist, first like dew, then like a soft summer rain, he said, "Watch for a waterfall. I didn't see it last time, but it should be where this meadow stream breaks over the ledge."

"I see it!" Suzanne ran ahead to the fern-ringed basin and lifted her face to the crest of the fall where a rainbow arched through the mist against the trees and sky above.

"Now," Winthrop spoke huskily, "we'll climb to the

top." He helped her scramble over the slippery rock outcrop to the margin of the meadow. "Look!"

He watched Suzanne's eyes gather wonder as they swept across the green sun-warmed turf, lingered over the crystal-clear stream, rose to the sentinel pines, and brushed across the hills folding away to the silver loop of the Muskingum. Then he let out his breath. For himself, too, the magic was still there.

He strode deeper into the meadow. "Come on, Susu," he called over his shoulder. Then, when she stood beside him, he began to pace off a square. "Here's a good place for the cabin. We can use some of the planks from our boat. It won't be too hard to haul them up the slope. And we'll gather stones from the basin—" he nodded toward the waterfall— "for our chimney. There's timber a-plenty yonder for a split-rail fence. About there," he pointed, "you and Mrs. McKnight can make your garden and have larkspur and phlox as well as onions and cabbages. We'll put a colt in the pasture for Merry."

Suzanne nodded and continued for him, dreamily, "Honeysuckle festooning the fence and smelling so fragrant, stone bread in the oven—"

"Would you chance it?"

Suzanne dropped her head into her hand. "I—I can't! We can't!"

"Why?" Winthrop's voice was sharp.

Suzanne groped for words to make Winthrop understand. Finally she said simply, "If we agree to take this land, we agree that Father is dead, that he's not coming, that we'll never go on to Kentucky. It would be giving up."

Winthrop stiffened. "No one's giving up!" For a moment he considered adding that no girl in her right mind
would call fighting the odds of a Donation Tract quitting. He
turned silently, instead, went to the stream, and lowered his
face into the cooling water. Then he knew Suzanne was
right.

She had a strange way of seeing things clearly that
others could only dimly sense. Fragile as she appeared, she
had a way too of giving a fellow some of her sturdy spirit
when his own had worn threadbare. Though there was much
here with which to build a home, there was not Josiah who
had always been—still was—the indispensable foundation.

"All right," Winthrop said, rising and wiping his face
with the hem of his fringed hunting shirt. "We'll wait. And
don't worry for ourselves or Mrs. McKnight. We'll find
something just right, all around."

For land he could, indeed, be patient. But once more the
need to skim the hills and burrow deep into the hollows in
search of his father swept over him with burning urgency.
Now that spring had come, work was going on in the chief
out-settlements promoted by the directors of the Ohio Company. There was the place they were calling Belle Prairie,
or Belpre, "beautiful prairie lands" twelve miles below
Marietta on the Ohio, opposite the mouth of the Little
Kanawha River; there was the cluster of cabins on Duck
Creek, to the east of the Muskingum and on the west, the
beginning of a settlement near the falls of Wolf Creek
where, too, a grist and sawmill would be erected. Plainfield,
nearby, was well under way.

He must volunteer his services in these places, he supposed, but cabin-raisings and corn-plantings interested him less than the surveying journeys. Somewhere deep in the forest or along an old Indian trail, he might find some clue to the fate of his father. There would probably be no extensive surveying expeditions for the present; the season was over. The time for that sort of work was when autumn winds had swept the hardwood trees bare of leaves or before spring sunshine and showers had brought the trees into foliage once more. Sighting was then easier for workers with the delicate instruments; chainbearers were less likely to find themselves suddenly sprawling in a sink-hole or pit, having been deceived by the dense foliage of thicket and underbrush covering it.

"We shall find something just right," he repeated.

CHAPTER THIRTEEN

Opportunity for a surveying trip came earlier than Winthrop expected—before the summer was over, in fact. Rumor had it that General Harmar intended to withdraw the troops from the fort that bore his name at the mouth of the Muskingum, and establish new headquarters downriver. One of his staff was already drawing up plans for a new fort to be named for President Washington and to be located opposite the Licking River's mouth. The time for which they had enlisted would soon be up for some of the soldiers and they had decided to purchase land and make their own settlement on the Ohio Company's lands. To have it ready for early occupancy, John Matthews and his surveying party, accompanied by a guard from Fort Harmar and hunters to keep them supplied with meat, had set off.

Now, three weeks later, Winthrop sat on the Ohio shore, fifteen miles below the Great Kanawha, waiting for a supply boat due from Marietta. It was good to rest awhile in the shade. During the three weeks the surveyors had been out on range number sixteen, they had struggled through steaming thickets, vines that held like giant tentacles, and dense forest littered with fallen trees. The nights had brought little relief from gnats and other insects, or from the oppressive August heat. Many a camp had been pitched by a dry stream.

After two of the packhorses laden with provisions had been lost in the woods, the party had lived a week on meat alone, and that of a very poor quality. Then the camp hunter had quit, remarking that no one could do better, since Indians had recently hunted over the territory. Winthrop had hoped that these Indian hunters might be Delawares, but the guard had grumbled, "Mingo, and well on their way south into the Scioto country by now." The trip had been tedious, and fruitless in his search for his father.

When Matthews announced his decision to give up and not complete the survey, Winthrop, like everyone, was glad enough to take to the boats at the Great Kanawha without question. They had gone toward the Muskingum as far as Old Town Creek, when they were met by the Ohio Company officials in the contractor's boat exploring and taking the course of the river to the end of the Company's purchase.

Winthrop could see by Matthews' visible wrath, as he stood in conversation with the officers, that there was a sharp disagreement about Matthews' decision to abandon for the present both surveying and exploring activities. Winthrop could not help overhearing some of what was said.

"Anyone would think you were in the special employ of certain of the Ohio Company agents back in Massachusetts and Connecticut. They do not want the boundary survey completed, of course."

"They don't? I do not understand!" Matthews' surprise was genuine. "Why?"

"At the time of their so-called purchase they made only a nominal down payment; the balance was to be due as soon as the survey had been completed."

160

"Yes, yes, I knew that." Matthews was impatient.

"Mr. Ludlow was employed to do the northern boundary. He went out from Wheeling with his party in March and returned in June—entirely unmolested by the Indians, by the way—with his part completed. Now the easterners are panicky. They are afraid the final boundary will be done and they will have to pay up."

"But don't they want to pay up? The settlers who were having them act as their agents gave them their money, their soldiers' bounties' papers or whatever was necessary, so they could have their warranty deeds from the government, in place of a mere contract, at the earliest possible moment. Don't they want to pay up?"

The other laughed, cynically. "Perhaps they would, if they had the money. Not all of them, but certain very influential ones thought there was going to be plenty of time. They have speculated with their clients' money and have lost it. Now they are suggesting everything possible to prevent the final survey being completed or, if it is completed, the acceptance of the surveyors' reports when presented."

"They—they wouldn't stoop to—" A sudden thought seemed to strike Matthews with horror. Already the thought had come to Winthrop's mind.

"To inciting the Indians to do a little molesting? Oh, no, I don't know that they would do that. Certainly they wouldn't encourage bloodshed. They wouldn't stoop to that — But I just thought possibly you might have had a little extra urging—" His sentence ended as a question. "To quit?"

Matthews' eyes were ablaze with a fire that did not fit

161

the coolness of his level voice. "My decision to leave the woods was based upon my judgment of the facts as then known: the lack of supplies and the unlikelihood that the situation would improve. Will you now promise, before going further downstream, to detach messengers to return to Marietta and order down provisions and at least two more packhorses?"

The officials conferred together very briefly and so promised.

"We return to the survey, men. We shall rendezvous at the encampment we made night before last." Matthews waved them toward the boats and they moved without delay.

Now, as Winthrop awaited the supply boat, many things went through his mind. With luck, range number sixteen could be charted by the end of another week. He suspected that if Anselm hadn't been busy with other affairs, had been able to be with the party, the range would already be plotted. Four or five weeks was a long time to be away from Suzanne and Merry. What if the stranger from the East had already arrived to oust them all from Mrs. McKnight's quarters in Campus Martius?

He rose impatiently, untethered the two packhorses nodding in the heat, and led them to the river to drink.

Later in the morning the supply boat, an awkward barge of about forty-ton burthen with a small cabin in the stern, came around the bend. Winthrop went to the edge of the shore and signaled the best approach. After the prow grated over the pebble beach, two men stood in argument on the foredeck, ignoring Winthrop.

"Orders is orders," one was saying, a big-framed, bare-chested man. "I'll unload for ye, but I want no more part of it. You heard what the messenger said. Matthews suspects the Indians are watching the surveyors' every move. That means they're watching us, too."

"Let 'em watch! I've told you," snapped the other, a bandy-legged, wiry man with graying hair, "I'm paid by the Ohio Company to deliver supplies. Well," he glared up at the big man, "unload them! We're behind schedule already."

Under the foreman's sullen direction the crew lost little time in carrying the supplies ashore, leading the packhorses along the teetering improvised gangplank to join their droop- ing fellows on the bank, and themselves going on down- stream.

Winthrop quickly lashed the supplies to the horses' backs and turned to retrace the route he had marked from camp. The boatmen's argument still burned in his ears. Lead- horse bridle in hand, he stepped softly, looking from side to side, but saw no one watching him from the long secret shadows of the forest.

He found the encampment along the run a few miles farther up the valley than the morning site. Eight soldiers of the guard were lounging in moody silence, cleaning their guns in the waning afternoon sunlight. Corporal Van Berckle, Private Mason, and two others were playing an indifferent game with soiled, dog-eared cards. Even the tire- less John Matthews and his assistant Sam Patchen had re- turned early.

Winthrop unloaded the packhorses, staked them out in a nearby grove, and silently went to work kindling a fire. Soon the smell of food, such as the party had not tasted in days, drifted through the camp, and the men began to stir and show some interest in fixing shelters into which they could crawl if the thunderstorm blew their way during the night. By the time Winthrop finished passing out their rations of hot grog, talk was again flowing freely.

"If one of us soldiers had been arrested, what kind of a sentence would he get?" Corporal Van Berckle teased, holding his tin cup to Winthrop for refilling. "One hundred lashes and a day in the stocks. But Master Lake, arrested by *Hetuck* himself, what does he get? By the double crown of my head, I wager it was naught but a rap on the knuckles! Even less than that?" He shook his shaggy head sadly. "So much for civil justice!"

Everyone laughed, but not unkindly. This was going to be a good meal. Private Mason grabbed the corporal by the hair playfully. "Better start wagering on something else, Dutch. Some red warrior will have your scalp yet. When split into its two crowns, it'll bring a double price, and the British none the wiser."

The corporal smoothed his mane. "It is not mine they are really wanting. I am only a soldier and on the right side of the river. The Indians hate longknife Virginians and you surveyor-people the most. Why else do you suppose two horses loaded with supplies disappeared?"

Sam Patchen leveled cold eyes on the corporal. "They wandered into the woods and were lost."

A bearded soldier of the guard sharpened his bayonet and squinted down its length. "Let's hope that is all that gets lost. The fresh signs I've been seein' points to ambush."

164

"The Indians have yet to molest any of us with whom they entered treaty," John Matthews said shortly.

"Yeah." The bearded soldier did not look at him. "But the signs I've been readin' spell Shawnee. The Shawnee didn't come to the treaty at Harmar."

John Matthews considered this in silence. There had indeed been more reason than the loss of supplies behind his decision to return to the Muskingum. The bearded soldier was right. Fresh signs did point to Shawnees, uncomfortably close. But he could not go against the orders of his superiors—nor again give them cause to suspect he was intentionally abandoning the survey for some personal gain.

Quietly he gave instructions. He would set out early in the morning with Sam Patchen and a guard of four soldiers. Corporal Van Berckle and Private Mason would join them during the day with the baggage. Winthrop should arrive at their new campsite by forenoon with the four packhorses of supplies.

A few drops of rain spattered down. Matthews ordered Winthrop to smother the cook fire with a large cut of sod. "Things are hot enough here without it," he said softly.

As Winthrop followed Matthews' trail the next morning he whistled off-key, uncomfortably aware that he led only three packhorses instead of four. He tried to persuade himself that Corporal Van Berckle and Private Mason, who were to bring on the baggage, would have the missing horse—one of the new ones—located by now. Then the thought that a war party had crept into the nearby grove during the night and stolen the horse while all slept in their blankets chilled him. Nevertheless, when he found John Matthews waiting at the noonday rendezvous, he was a little taken aback by the sharpness of his question.

"Where is the rest of the party?"

"They should be along any time now. I left them beating the woods for the other packhorse."

Matthews sighed. "Sit down, Winthrop." He picked up a twig and began to sketch in the damp earth. "You're not easily panicked, are you? I hope not, for it will be neces-sary for me to leave you here alone to wait for the soldiers with the baggage. Now, a question. How well did you tether that horse?"

Winthrop looked at his companion squarely. "I don't want to make it look as if the fault wasn't possibly mine, sir. But I did tie that horse especially securely, because she was new to the night woods. Of course, with the thunder and lightning to frighten her, she might very well have bucked and reared enough to pull up the stake."

"I don't think so." Matthews pointed to the lines he had made on the ground. "This morning when I was crossing this creek running from the northwest I found the tracks of three horses traveling up the stream. They had passed since the rain of last night. Two of the tracks are of unshod ponies, probably Indian. The third is shod with the type of shoe used at Fort Harmar."

Winthrop felt a prickling sensation at the back of his neck.

Matthews eyed him blankly. "Now what do you say?"

Winthrop wet his lips. "I say let them have it."

"Good. You may make a tolerable surveyor yet." He

166

rose and began to gather his equipment. "I have sent Sam Patchen to scout a little farther to be sure the Indians are leaving this section. I must get back to the line, as I left the guard holding the chain and there's no telling where they'll have it by now. When the others come, detain them in camp."

Winthrop stared after Matthews until he was out of sight around the bend in the run. When he moved to the cover of the brush, he told himself it was to keep out of the heat. But he soon gave up all pretense and sat with his musket cocked across his knees. He found himself shaking with relief when the horsemen coming down the wooded side of the ravine turned out to be Corporal Van Berckle and Private Mason with the baggage. The packhorse had not been found.

The corporal frowned as he listened to Winthrop's account of Matthews' findings. "Time was we would have chased the Indians and got our horse back. Now, by the treaty, first we notify them of our hostile intentions, *ja*?" He dusted his breeches with his cap.

"Don't forget," Mason said, as he reined in his horse and swung to the ground, "both whites and Indians agreed to give up hoss thieving in the first place."

"So we sit here and wait for them to leave the country." Corporal Van Berckle stretched lazily. "Times are changing."

One by one the men began to straggle in. By evening all had returned except Sam Patchen. Everyone found something to do and worked in silence, avoiding each other's eyes. And each one stole uneasy glances into the darkening forest. Nothing was said about putting out the fire, and the corporal to all appearances accidentally discharged his musket while cleaning it.

It was dark when Sam Patchen finally came into camp, winded, at a brisk trot. They gathered about him in an anxious circle and listened to what he had to report.

"I followed the trail of a man and a horse passing over the valley in which we camped yesterday," he panted. "It joined the trail of the three horsemen Mr. Matthews discovered this morning."

"Good," Matthews commented. "One less to worry about."

Sam Patchen shook his head. "As the trail led on up the creek it ran into the tracks of eight or ten more horsemen, and moccasin tracks of a few more men traveling on foot."

The soldiers began to talk all at once.

"Sounds like a plundering party has been over to the old settlement on the Great Kanawha."

"Or to the new one on the Sandy River."

"And on their way back stole the horse and are hittin' now fer tall timber, before we can ketch 'em."

John Matthews' voice cut through the confusion. "Did any of the tracks double back?"

"No." Sam Patchen was obviously relieved. "At least, none that I could tell."

The corporal stroked his chin. "But they could."

Matthews rose abruptly. "Corporal, you will station sentries at regular intervals surrounding our position. Each man will take a post as I direct, here in camp. If he falls asleep, let it be with his arms ready. You all know Indians usually attack at daybreak. Before that time we will turn out under arms. You understand this is—a necessary precaution."

The alerting of the surveyors and guard left Winthrop with the impression that Matthews was taking more than a necessary precaution. But his own assignment was an inglorious one—guarding the remaining packhorses staked now near the sod-smothered campfire in the safe, inner circle of the picket.

Long before nightfall Winthrop sat with his back to a stump, blinking away the sleep that settled occasionally over him. All around was darkness. He gazed intently into the black, tensing as he made out a grayish figure passing beyond the creek. After a while he saw the shape return with measured pace and knew it was only a sentry. Then he sat bolt upright. He had a sudden sharp sense of being trapped. What protection was that small grayish figure? It was pacing off a perfect target for the enemy who watched from the hills all about them! Winthrop did not want to die this way. He could not! As clearly as if Josiah were out there in the fog, Winthrop, remembering, heard him say, "Take care of your sisters!" Then Winthrop had a vision of Suzanne as she had stood at the brink of the meadow, eyes filling with wonder. He recalled Merry, sitting on the hearth in the firelight, one dimpled arm turning the handle of the music box. Then he saw his father as a captive of the Delawares, his small, gallant frame bent by savage slavery. He bit his lips and sat in grim silence, musket cocked, waiting for the hour before dawn.

It was about four-thirty, Winthrop reckoned, when a robin somewhere in a thicket began a persistent chirp that filed against his overwrought nerves. It was still quite dark, though a faint gray streak began to widen over the eastern hills. Even before John Matthews spoke a low command, the camp was astir. The soldiers of the guard were checking their bullet pouches and guns and drawing into rank. Corporal Van Berckle, fastening on his sword, moved up and down the small column giving orders. Sam Patchen, sitting near Winthrop, shook so that he could hardly pull on his boots. "Nothing's going to cheat me out of my donation land," he was muttering to no one in particular. "See? Here's the grant in my pocket."

Winthrop watched the men spread into a widening circle and melt into the heavy fog. In spite of orders, sitting inside the circle and guarding old horses was unthinkable! He snatched up his musket, ran after John Matthews, and tapped him on the shoulder. Matthews turned sharply.

"Please!" Winthrop begged.

"All right, then." Matthews nodded curtly. "Station yourself a rod from my post behind that bush."

The bush looked like a crouching monster in the swirling fog, but Winthrop felt his way across the rough ground and there took up his stand. Though he knew Matthews was within easy hailing distance in the thicket and Private Mason only another rod away, concealed behind a rotted stump, he felt he was alone, facing an enemy he could not see.

After what seemed an eternity of trying to hear an alien sound in the sounds of the waking forest, to see through the lifting mist and lightening gray a stealthy figure that might be behind the next bush, or the next, daylight came. The sun grew warm, then hot, and perspiration trickled be-

170

"Glad it was a false alarm after all," Matthews said

tween Winthrop's shoulder blades. Still nothing happened. Finally Matthews stepped into sight and said in a normal voice, "Start the word around the circle, Winthrop. Abandon posts for camp." Seeing Winthrop's haggard face, he grinned. "Glad it was a false alarm after all."

Winthrop walked, with legs suddenly gone weak, to Private Mason's post and spoke with a tongue strangely thick. "It's all up," he said, feeling an odd sense of unreality.

"You don't say!" Private Mason kept staring into the forest. Then, with an air of uncertainty, he lifted his gun from the prop on the rotted stump. "Still, it's the habit of the Injuns to strike at dawn if they're going to, and sunup's near two hours past." He turned to look at Winthrop.

"Matthews says to send the word on to return to camp."

"Dutch is in yon ravine." With another sharp glance into the forest, Mason turned and led the way, scratching his side.

The corporal came out to meet them, his round face unsmiling. "I got already the word. I don't like it. Things are too quiet. These surveyors have not a soldier's nose for trouble."

Winthrop's loyalty to the surveyors struggled with his own unpleasant sense of something still wrong. "Matthews was in the Ohio country before there was ever a Fort Harmar," he said.

"Spunky!" The corporal's broad face broke into a smile. "But done in, *ja*? And breakfast yet to get. Mason, we fetch for him water from the spring to lighten his labors."

"You can lighten my arms of this musket now," Winthrop said, handing it to Mason, "while I gather firewood."

The two soldiers went toward the spring nearby in the hillside and Winthrop circled to a hickory grove south of camp where the wind had broken off the dry limbs. Arms loaded, he lengthened his stride as he saw through the trees that almost everyone was back at the campsite, lounging in the sun in the open stretch near the creek. Some were already pounding their knives against their messkits in a clamor for breakfast. Sam Patchen, Winthrop observed with a smile, as he drew closer, was sitting again on his blanket, boots off, studying the grant to his hundred acres of donation land.

Winthrop heard the gun shot crack out before he saw the look of surprise on Patchen's face, or saw him clutch his shirt where the blood began to spurt through his fingers. "I'm shot!" Patchen cried in a strangled voice. Then he fell over and lay with an open-eyed stare at the sky.

For an instant no one moved. Then the bearded soldier drinking at the stream shouted, "Ambush! Ambush!" before another shot sent him sprawling into the stream.

Winthrop dropped the wood and fumbled for his gun before he realized he had given it to Mason. At the same time every man in camp was scrambling to his feet, frantically snatching up muskets or any weapon at hand. "Where are the shots coming from?" a bewildered young soldier cried in a shrill voice. The answer was a volley of bullets and arrows seeming to come from everywhere.

Three men, half rising, fell in a grotesque heap. The packhorse screamed and bit at the arrow in its ribs. A soldier, fixing his bayonet, pitched forward onto the blade. Another hoarsely cried, "Charge, charge, you cowards!" to a knot of men crawling toward the baggage for cover.

Then Winthrop saw the Shawnee leap into sight through the woods at the opposite side of the camp. They came running, splashing through the creek, muskets thrown aside for tomahawks, knives, and spears, closing in with high-pitched yells for the kill. One on the right flank paused to pick up a compass, examine it curiously, and whoop with glee before he flung a tomahawk with terrible accuracy at a soldier taking aim. Another warrior wrenched the gun from a soldier's bleeding hand and smashed it against a tree.

For Winthrop, with no weapons, concealment was the only protection. He bent low and began to run, not daring to stop, though branches lashed his face and shoulders and briars tore cruelly at his legs. His heart thudded heavily against his ribs as he suspected, then was certain, that someone was following him. Finally, unable to bear it longer, he snatched up a heavy stick, plunged blindly into a patch of briars, and turned to look.

It was John Matthews! Winthrop stumbled over a log and lay there, gasping with relief. "We can't stop now!" Matthews panted, scarcely pausing.

Winthrop struggled to his feet and followed. "Patchen?" he managed to ask.

"Dead," Matthews answered, "and we will be too if we don't keep going. Head for the river and the exploring party. It's our only chance!"

"Are you hurt?" Winthrop called.

For answer, Matthews jerked his head toward a bullet hole in the full part of his sleeve. "Just missed."

It seemed to Winthrop that it took hours for them to work their way over the hills, along ridges, and into dry vales until they found again a stream leading riverward.

Matthews wiped the sweat from his face. "We've come only eight miles! Surveyed this spot a week ago." It was the most he had spoken during their grim journey. He sank to the bank and sat looking at his bare feet, swollen, torn, and bleeding. "A fine time I picked to call off the sentry!" he choked. "And to be caught without my boots on."

Winthrop swallowed hard. This was not the time to remind Matthews that his men had been sent back to the range against his advice and better judgment, he decided. Instead, he inquired, "How far is it to the river?"

Matthews did not appear to hear.

Matthews started to tie the soft deerskin strips on his ankles

Winthrop peeled off his hunting shirt and began to slash it into strips. "The going will be easier if you bind up those feet."

Matthews carefully lowered his feet into the cool stream, dried them, and tied the soft deerskin strips about his ankles. "About three miles to the river," he answered at last. Then he rose, and before setting out again, turned to Winthrop, eyes rimmed with weariness and defeat. "Do you know—did you see—what happened to Mason and Van Berckle?"

Winthrop wet his lips. "No. They went to the spring for water. Maybe they got away, too," he added with a forlorn hope.

By the time they neared the marshland and saw the river shining ahead, Matthews could barely walk. All the heart seemed to have gone out of him. Winthrop beat a path through the sharp reeds at the edge of the swamp and led the way along a grassy ledge to the shore.

They sat wearily on a driftlog. Matthews pointed to a stake driven into a mound of earth at the creek mouth. "Thirty-mile post. Fresh broken ground. Probably set yesterday." He lapsed into silence, as if to think further were too great an effort.

"Then the contractor's boat can't be very far away."

"Too far to swim," Matthews replied heavily. "You'd better go on. Follow the shoreline, but keep to cover of the trees."

Winthrop pretended not to notice Matthews' hopelessness. "And leave you to your brooding and who knows what!" Winthrop thought. "Ah, no!" A sudden idea struck him. He took hold of Matthews' arm and shook it. "See here! If we can make a raft of these driftlogs, laced with tough grapevine, we might yet catch up with the contractor's boat."

"Yes?" Matthews' expression did not change, but he set to work with Winthrop.

The raft was half completed when Winthrop lifted his head to brush a mosquito from his face. He stood a moment gazing upriver, his eyes wide in disbelief. "Look!" He pointed with a trembling hand to the Kentucky boat that loomed around the bend under full power of oar and pole.

Matthews cupped his hands to call, but his voice failed him.

"Help!" Winthrop shouted.

He was answered by the clear blast of a boatman's horn as the keelboat swung toward shore. It was Corporal Van Berckle and Private Mason who helped them over the plank onto the deck. Matthews stood there a moment swaying, his joy at seeing the soldiers held back as he searched for the scorn that might be in their faces.

Van Berckle rubbed his thatch of yellow hair and grinned. "We cheated them out of my double-crowned scalp again, *ja?*"

"Faith!" Mason rolled his eyes. "All by going to fetch water for yon camp boy, we've saved our nightcaps. I vow it, never again will I make sport of him!"

Winthrop, watching Matthews, saw the slow smile come to his face.

The owner of the keelboat, a lanky man with a mane of sandy hair of his own, came forward. "Any more of you?"

Matthews' brows went up in a silent question.

The soldiers shook their heads grimly.

"Well—" the boatman spoke gruffly to hide his sympathy— "the current is running swift for this time of year. Reckon we might catch up with your other party before nightfall."

"Thanks. But it won't be necessary. We're going back ashore," Matthews said.

The boatman gaped. "What for?"

"To bury our dead."

Winthrop knew then that Matthews had won his own victory. He was in command once more, of others, and of himself.

177

CHAPTER FOURTEEN

"No! You may not go to the mounds. The Sabbath is not the time to romp." Mrs. McKnight chided Merry. "Besides, didn't you read the law posted on the birch tree that every able-bodied man, woman, and child is obliged to attend divine service? Of course, you can't read," she relented. "Just take my word for it, that's what it says." Hastily she scooped another portion of mush and milk into Merry's upheld noggin.

Merry, without tasting the mush, pushed the noggin aside on the table. Her face set rebelliously. "I want to go to the mounds," she insisted. She left the table, went to the trunk at the back of the room, lifted the music box from its top, and stood in silence hugging it against her.

"You dare not dig in the mounds, anyhow," the woman continued scolding. "The directors have set them aside for public parks, not to be molested."

Suzanne looked up from Merry's drab brown hood to which she was sewing a blue ribbon cockade. She had bartered a bushel of pawpaws from the woods to Captain Prince for the trimming. Some might think it a vanity. But the child did hunger for pretties. Suzanne suspected that it was for trinkets Merry wanted to search the mounds— arrowheads veined like autumn leaves, copper beads green with mold, and bright bits of pottery to add to her small hoard. Her fond glance went from Merry's rebellious pout to Widow McKnight's flushed face. Suzanne had learned that when the usually kindly woman was concerned about something her tongue was sharp. It was uncommonly sharp this morning.

"What treasure you expect to find at the mounds is beyond me, anyway," Mrs. McKnight concluded flatly, lifting the iron lid of the stew pot and vigorously stirring the simmering meat.

Suzanne opened her mouth to come to Merry's defense but changed her mind. Merry looked up into Mrs. Mc-Knight's face and spoke with the uncertain dignity of her few years. "I want to go to the big mound and play the music box so Papa might hear it and find his way out of the forest." She turned to Suzanne, her eyes dancing with sudden tears. "I heard you tell Winthrop once that when I played the music box on the boat it brought Papa back from a long way."

The spoon in Mrs. McKnight's hand clattered to the hearth.

Suzanne's throat tightened. She went swiftly to Merry and knelt at her side. "Such a beautiful tune! Would you play it for us now?"

Merry turned the handle slowly at first; then, reassured, turned it rapidly. She darted Mrs. McKnight a quick, forgiving smile.

The woman tried an answering smile and failed. She went to the window and stood looking out through a gray pane.

Suzanne whispered to Merry. "Be a pet and fetch my

cloak from the back room." As soon as Merry was out of sight, Suzanne quietly put the music box on top of the high corner cupboard where the little girl could not reach it and where she hoped it would lie forgotten for a while.

Mrs. McKnight, without turning, spoke to Suzanne across the silence. "Merry has grown from a toddler to a child with strong ideas of her own. Time has gone all too quickly." She sighed. "Who knows how long she has been hankering for her lost mother and father? I, with my thorny ways, have been a poor makeshift."

Suzanne began clearing the table, at a loss for a way to tell Mrs. McKnight that no one minded her sharp tongue, ever. "Are the supplies running short again?" she asked instead.

"That is of small concern. Anyone can face famine as long as he has shelter and others with whom to share privation." After a pause, she turned and said abruptly, "Suzanne, there's something I've been keeping from you." She came slowly to the table, pulled a letter from her deep apron pocket and laid it on the smooth-scrubbed boards. She took a deep breath. "You know how kind everyone has been to me—ever since Sergeant McKnight lost his life in the attack at the Falls. General Putnam arranged with the directors of the Ohio Company for me to occupy these quarters until such time as the rightful owner, a shareholder in the East, should come and claim them. That time will soon be here. We can live here but a few weeks longer. I've kept the matter from you as long as I could. Read the letter from General Putnam. It will explain all."

Suzanne picked up the folded sheet, glanced briefly

over the fine handwriting, and without reading it, handed it back. Her smile began deep in her eyes. "We've known since early Spring."

"What?" sputtered Mrs. McKnight. "How could you know? The owner's letter to General Putnam arrived only yesterday by way of a passing boat from Fort Pitt!"

Suzanne looked up timidly as if she had been guilty of eavesdropping. "I knew it was going to be happening. I overheard some women talking at the well."

Mrs. McKnight's face reddened. "Gossiping females! What is worse? I had hoped to spare you from further troubles, to provide security until the final day came —"

"We knew you had your own good reasons for not telling us," Suzanne interrupted softly.

Mrs. McKnight looked with resignation at her work-worn hands. "The Lord giveth and the Lord taketh away."

Suzanne began gathering up the pewter spoons from the table. "That same morning we heard, when Winthrop and I told you we were going for a picnic on the donation lands, remember? We looked at a place in the hills Winthrop fancies. He will ask for it soon—" she hesitated—"if Father isn't found."

"La!" exclaimed Mrs. McKnight. "I suspected something more than a lark that day!"

"There's rock nearby to build a fireplace big enough for you to bake stone bread, and a place for your garden, with flowers," Suzanne added hurriedly.

Mrs. McKnight dabbed at her eyes, at the same time trying to look severe. "No one has consulted me."

A moment later, just before the sundial in the square

shadowed ten o'clock, Merry rushed from the back room, hearing the drum call and the tread of booted feet through the gate. She stood on tiptoe holding up Suzanne's cloak. "Time to go." When Suzanne and Mrs. McKnight took no notice she looked wonderingly from face to face. "Time to go," she insisted, tugging at Suzanne's skirt.

"Why, yes, so it is!" Suzanne hurried to lift her bonnet from a wall-peg and, giving Mrs. McKnight no chance to say more, bent to tie Merry's hood under her chin. As they went to the doorway she tucked the child's curls into place. Suddenly aware that Mrs. McKnight was not beside them, she turned in surprise on the threshold. "Aren't you coming?"

"Mrs. Welsh is still too poorly to stir from her bed at the Point," Mrs. McKnight answered primly while over her face passed a flicker of guilt at Merry's accusing gaze. "Law or no law, I believe my Christian duty is with her."

Outside, Suzanne stood with Merry on the stone step, watching the crowd assemble to march to the meeting hall for the morning devotion. The drummer, a gangling freckled youth, beat the muster call; the militia drew into rank. A hush settled over the square when the command, "Present arms!" rang out. Muskets clattered and the inspecting officer's spurs clanked as he walked up and down the lines. Anselm stepped forward to call the roll. Suzanne stole a shy glance at him. Anselm had not yet assembled the correct uniform for his office as post major. He was wearing shabby, outgrown cavalry trousers topped by a fringed hunting shirt, but he wore them and his officer's saber and triangular hat jauntily.

While the soldiers stood at attention, Colonel Sproat strode forward and drew his sword. The drummer and the fifer, a short-legged man, fell in behind him, followed by the civil officers and the militia, the Reverend Daniel Story in his black robe, and the inhabitants in their sober Sunday dress. The drummer rolled out a smart beat, the fifer struck up an almost lively tune, and the column moved forward. Suzanne hastily led Merry to the group of children waiting outside a door. It was Mary Bird's house, where she held a Sabbath school for the young children of the settlement. Suzanne promised to stop by for Merry after the service, and took a place in the rear of the procession that marched into the meeting hall.

In the quiet pause, after the opening hymn, the Reverend Mr. Story stood looking over his congregation. He was tall, his slender shoulders somewhat widened by the wilderness canoe routes he was traveling on his circuit as chaplain for the Ohio Company. His long hands had been noticeably white against his black garb when first he had arrived from Massachusetts, in March of that year, 1789. Now they were brown and hard. But the wilderness had not hardened the gentle, radiant smile always hovering about his mouth, however much it had deepened the brown-eyed stare that seemed to search through a person toward his very soul. He fixed his gaze on the entire gathering.

"We should deal gently with the Indians," he said slowly, "for the sake of the Father of all. If we, having the light of the Sacred Word to guide us, persecute and oppress them, how great shall be our punishment! Let us beware that we err not."

Benches creaked and throats cleared protestingly. The Reverend Mr. Story continued, raising one finger to stress his point. "What is the first law? Love thy neighbor as thyself; honor all men as brothers—" He stopped mid-sentence, interrupted by a single loud creak of the door.

Suzanne looked discreetly from under her bonnet brim and saw Peter Nyswonger's shaggy head in the doorway, his huge, hairy hand motioning to the drummer who sat near the side entrance. The drummer drew his instrument from under the bench and went out.

Reverend Daniel Story saw the silent tableau also. "Let us beware that we err not—" he began again, but he faltered when the long beat of the drum rattled outside and the four-pounder cannon boomed from the northeast bastion. The little congregation looked momentarily to the parson as if to ask him if they had heard rightly, whether it was indeed the signal that hostile Indians were nearby. White-faced, he raised his hand in dismissal and in blessing. "The Lord watch over us all."

In an instant the quiet room was in an uproar. The militia clambered over their benches toward their muskets stacked in the rear. The aging officers of the War for Independence forgot their retirement and bawled orders no one heeded. A woman caught up her cloak, wrapped it protectively about her baby, and stumbled blindly toward the doorway. Others did not even wait to catch up their cloaks.

Suzanne leaped to her feet with the single purpose of finding Merry. She pushed her way along the noisy passage, darted through a group of militia running to take up their posts at the sentry boxes, past three young men striding toward the sally port with long pikes in hand, and stopped breathlessly at Mary Bird's door.

Mrs. Bird stood in the open doorway, calm and erect. "Line up, children," she ordered quietly. "Those of you who live here within the stockade file out one by one and go straight to your own doors. The others will remain with me until the alarm is over."

Suzanne stood aside as the children came out, capering with excitement. Merry was not among them. Mrs. Bird turned to close the door. "Wait!" Suzanne cried and ran forward, peering into the dim room. Three children were sitting on a high chest, and two very small ones on the bed. "Merry?" she managed to ask. The woman turned to her, concern now in every line of her face. "Merry has not been here this morning. I thought she had gone to worship with you."

Suzanne forced herself to speak evenly. "Don't worry. She's probably home right now." She turned and ran through the crowded square, pushed open the unlatched door, and called into the familiar kitchen. "Merry?" She stood listening. "Merry?" This time she called sharply. "Are you hiding? This is no time to play games!"

The fire had gone out; the leaden sky had grown darker; from the doorway it was hard to see anything in the kitchen, and the back room was a silent pool of shadows.

Suzanne's mind flew back to Merry's rebellious face. Had she gone to the big mound, after all? If so, there wasn't a minute to lose. She fought down panic and hurried toward the black-bearded sentry who stood at the main gate answering two men who questioned as they passed, carrying a box

185

of ammunition from the guardhouse. "Yes, Nyswonger found plenty fresh moccasin tracks up on his place at Duck Creek. Nine hills of potatoes dug and stole, a fat hog killed and carried off."

A few hungry Indians, not a war party! And Nyswonger's claim was a long way from the mound. Suzanne slumped with relief.

"Fresh sign this morning, other side of the mound beyond the cornfield," the sentry went on in his nasal voice. "Looked like the tracks of an Indian spy, circling and watching. No telling how many's waiting behind him."

Suzanne stiffened with fear. She went up to the sentry and asked, "Did a little girl go outside less than an hour ago?"

The sentry took off his hat and scratched his head, the better to remember. "More than a few folks was coming and going then. At that time I didn't have no call to be too watchful."

"A little red-headed girl with a blue ribbon on her hood?" Suzanne pressed.

The sentry's mouth screwed up in thought, then broke into a grin. "Oh, sure! The young 'un at the Widow McKnight's. I recollect she went out a short spell after the widow. Reckon they'll be in together any minute, 'less they forted up at the Point." He squinted toward the road winding through the woodland and into the clearing. "Here come some folks now."

Suzanne raced out the gate without waiting to hear more.

"Come back, Miss! Come back!" shouted the guard.

186

Suzanne went up to the sentry

Suzanne lowered her head and ran the faster across the clearing and onto the road entering the forest. She almost collided with the blacksmith who was hurrying along to safety, his leather apron full of tools and tobacco. "Did you see Merry with Mrs. McKnight at the Point?" Suzanne cried. The blacksmith shook his head mutely and went on. "Have you seen Merry?" she asked a woman who came next dragging a feather tick with one hand and holding with the other to her child. "Merry?" the woman asked dazedly. "Merry *who*?" Suzanne ran on to question a young girl carrying a china teapot and a large Bible. The girl stared at her blankly and without answering turned to call over her shoulder, "Hurry, hurry, Grandma!" The elderly lady hobbled up, shaking her head and muttering, "Savages or not, I couldn't have them find the house looking so!" They went on, leaving Suzanne alone on the road.

It was very still, now that the road ahead was empty. Spits of snow drove through the overhanging trees and blew along the ruts ahead. To the east beyond the cornfield that rustled drily in the rising wind loomed the mound top. If Merry had gone on down the road after Mrs. McKnight, chances were they would be safely together in the block-house at the Point. But if Merry had gone to the mound where the fresh Indian tracks circled, she might be cringing there, afraid to call, or worse still, playing, unmindful of her danger. Suzanne measured with her eye the shortest way through the cornfield. "Best not to look back," she thought, but before she pushed aside the first of the dead stalks to plunge into the field she glanced over her shoulder. The blacksmith had slowed to a walk and was carrying the feather tick belonging to the woman with the child. The girl with the china teapot and the Bible was helping her grandmother along across the clearing. "Wait for us! Let us in!" the old woman shrilled as the main gate began slowly to close.

Bending low to keep out of sight, pulling her cloak close about her to fend off the sharp, slashing leaves, turning and twisting to steal as silently as possible through the close-planted stalks, Suzanne blundered her way into the field. The dried corn tassels clutched at her like skeleton fingers. The mud-clods clung to her shoes as if to pull her back. Still, when she reached the margin of the plain, she shrank back, dreading to leave cover.

The open plain ahead had never looked so wide, nor had the mound rising beyond ever seemed so distant. Fear froze her as she hesitated. To break into the open might mean an arrow or a flung spear in her back. She gasped and crouched lower among the cornstalks. Then the thought of Merry brought her upright with a start. She took a deep breath and ran, thinking of nothing but the desperate need of reaching the brush at the base of the mound. Cape flying, she raced over the frosty ground, stumbled over a hillock, swerved around a mossy log, and ducked into the shelter of the tangled thicket. She straightened and listened. There was a stealthy rustling among the twigs ahead. A chill of fear ran down her spine. She began to breathe again when she saw it was only a small rabbit.

With an effort she forced herself to stop trembling. "I can't be afraid, I can't stop now," she urged herself, then slipped over the side of the moat into the deep-piled leaves.

She scrambled to her feet and began to climb up the steep slope, holding to saplings and digging her fingers into matted tufts of grass and ferns. At last she topped the mound. She set her back to a maple tree trunk and looked all about. Nothing on the plain below, nothing on the road, nothing she could see through the treetops that stretched like a black, tossing sea toward Duck Creek. But there, caught on a bramble halfway down the other side of the mound, was a flutter of blue! The ribbon from Merry's hood!

"Merry!" Her voice was distorted with fear, hope.

The sound of something crackling through the forest and snapping the twigs of the thicket beyond the mound came up to her. Then she saw the blurred outline of a horseman making his way through the canebrake toward the rim of the moat directly below her. Suzanne pressed closer to the tree and slipped to the other side.

"Suzanne! Where are you? Suzanne!"

Anselm's voice. Tears of relief stung her eyes. "Up here!"

Anselm swung from the horse, leaped the moat, and ran up the mound. "Are you all right?" he asked before he reached her. "The sentry told me you'd gone out. I've looked everywhere for you!"

"I'm all right," she answered unsteadily. "It's Merry." She pointed to the bit of blue ribbon on the brambles. "She's been here but now she's gone. She might be anywhere, and with the Indians about—"

"The Indians left shortly before that alarm was sounded. Both scouts in the east sector report watching them pass," Anselm told her reassuringly. He took Suzanne's arm to help her down the slope. "Merry is at Mrs. McKnight's."

"Then no harm has come to her?" The color began to come back to Suzanne's face. Impulsively her hand tightened on Anselm's arm; then she drew away, blushing.

Anselm lifted Suzanne to the saddle and swung up behind her. They rode for a minute in silence until Anselm began carefully, "Merry is with Mrs. McKnight—yes. But she is somewhat dazed and has what seems to be a bad bump on her head. Mrs. McKnight quickly located Dr. True when she found her there—on the floor—at home. The doctor says it is nothing that time and rest and Epsom salts bandages will not cure," he added hurriedly before his companion could interrupt. "Merry must have fallen trying to reach something on the cupboard. There was a trunk, a stool, and the overturned churn in a pile beside her."

"Oh, the poor little girl! She was after the music box!" Suzanne gasped, seeing all too clearly with her mind's eyes Merry climbing, reaching, straining, teetering, and falling. "I put it out of reach this morning. It's all my fault. Oh, let's hurry!"

"Accidents are no one's fault," Anselm reminded Suzanne softly, remembering the day she had told him the same thing in her own way by the simple offer of a fresh-baked loaf of bread. Now all he could do was to set his spurs lightly to the horse, hold tightly to Suzanne's waist, and set off at a gallop for the stockade.

Suzanne swept past the silent group in the back room and went straight to Merry's bedside.

Merry turned her head. Her dazed eyes seemed to be asking Suzanne to bend down. Suzanne answered their mute message; she leaned nearer. Merry whispered, "I didn't mind you. I fell, trying to put the music box back."

Suzanne gently touched Merry's bandaged forehead, unable to speak.

"You won't care that I didn't mind you when I tell you—" Suddenly Merry smiled brightly. "I played the music box to bring Papa out of the forest. He didn't come—" Her voice trailed off, then rallied as Suzanne bent even closer. "But Silverheels did. He told me—he's found Papa—" Her eyes clouded again.

Dr. True stepped forward, motioning for Suzanne to leave the bedside.

Suzanne ignored the doctor. "Merry, say it again," she pleaded. "Silverheels has found our father?"

"Yes." Merry smiled like a happy child whose faith in all good things has been rewarded. Her eyes closed and she slept.

Looking down at her, Suzanne felt her own faith and hope surging back, though so many uncertainties remained. She wondered how and where her father was. She wondered if Silverheels was seeking to get word to Winthrop. She would, herself, try to reach her brother in a few days—as soon as she felt she could leave Merry's bedside.

CHAPTER FIFTEEN

Winthrop woke with a start, trying at one and the same time to get his bearings in the unfamiliar room and to trace the sound that had awakened him. Moonbeams slanted from a high window and pointed to a grotesque shape in the far corner. From outside came the sound of falling water. He sat erect and rubbed his eyes. His vision cleared. The shape in the corner, he now saw, was a huge grain hopper made from the shell of a length of hollow sycamore stump. The water he heard was Wolf Creek flowing over its solid limestone bed to the rapids and breaking over the fall. He was at Wolf Creek Mills, already so named although the millstones themselves had not yet arrived by flatboat from the Laurel Mountain region of Pennsylvania. He had spent the day adjusting the rest of the machinery awaiting their reception. If all went well, they would be able to grind a bushel of corn or rye into fine meal in four minutes. He had fallen asleep waiting for the guard to return from Waterford to stand watch.

His mind swung back to the sound that had startled him. There had been something stealthy about it. He sat still and listened. Someone was coming across the narrow footbridge that spanned the creek to the mill door. He did not hear the footfalls. Rather, he felt a very slight vibration of the bridge cables along the floor planking. He snatched

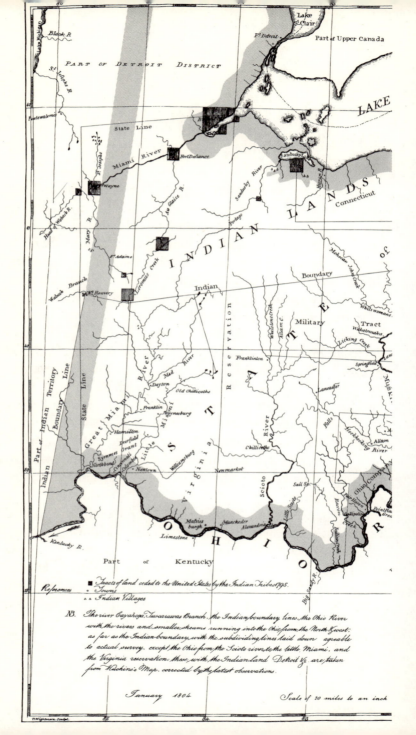

Lake St. Clair

Ft. Detroit

Part of Upper Canada

Lake Michigan

Black R.

PART OF DETROIT DISTRICT

St. Josephs R.

LAKE

Powtewatemie

State Line

Miami River

Ft. Joseph

Fort Defiance

Sandusky L.

Ft. Wayne

Au Glaize R.

Sandusky River

Portage

INDIAN LANDS

Connecticut

Mohican John's Creek

Ft. Adams

Hurd Wabash R.

Wabash Branch

St. Mary R.

Ft. Recovery

Caracatis Creek

Indian

Reservation

Boundary

White womans

of

Wellencreek

Allum C.

Military

Tract

Wakatomaka

Licking Creek

Springfield

MUSK

Franklinton

Part of Indian Territory Line

Indian Boundary Line

State Line

Great Miami River

Mad River

Miami River

Dayton

Old Chillicothe

Franklin

Waynsburgh

Mohican

River

V i r g i n i a

S T A T E

Mohican John's Creek

Lancaster

Falls

Hockhocking River

Allum River

Hamilton

Deerfield

Symmes Grant

Northbend Covington

Columbia

Newtown

Williamsburgh

Newmarket

Scioto River

Reservation

Chillicothe

Salt Sp.

Ohio Consp.

Big Hocking

Gallipolis

Printing

Kentucky R.

Malvies burgh

Limestone

Manchester

Alexandria

O H I O

Salt Sp.

Little Scioto R.

Raccoon

Indian Creek

Big Sandy R.

Printy Great

Part of Kentucky

O H I O R.

■ Tracts of land ceded to the United States by the Indian Tribes 1795.
○ Towns
▲▲ Indian Villages

References

NB. The river Cayahoga. Tuscarawas Branch. the Indian boundary lines. the Ohio River with the rivers and smaller streams running into the Ohio from the North & west: as far as the Indian boundary. with the subdividing lines laid down agreable to actual survey. except the Ohio from the Scioto river, to the little Miami. and the Virginia reservation: those, with the Indian land Detroit &c. are taken from Hutchins's Map. corrected by the latest observations.

January 1804

Scale of 20 miles to an inch

T. Wightman. Sculpt.

This is a map of the state of Ohio, as it was drawn by Rufus Putnam in January, 1804, including his misspellings! To this map only three things have been added: the location of Fort Harmar, the location of Duck Creek, and an indication of the territory covered by the Northwest Territory of Ohio, shown by the tinted edge.

up his musket and moved swiftly across the room to the rear window. Carefully he pushed the shutters open and dropped to the ground.

Keeping to the shadow of the mill he inched his way along the siding and peered around the corner. The clearing in front of the mill and the bridge reaching beyond to the dark forest were empty in the moonlight. He did not hear the soft scuff of moccasined feet behind him until it was too late and his arms were pinned to his side. The hands that held him tightened momentarily, then released him. "You smart like *Mugwa,* the bear. Should be smart like *Wawa kotchethe,* the fox," said a gruff voice.

Winthrop wheeled, his eyes wide open with shock, his mouth open with astonishment. "Silverheels!" Even in the shadows there was no mistaking him, though he had shaved his head, leaving only a tightly braided scalp lock on top in the manner of the forest Indian who must travel through brambles and underbrush. His long leggings worked with quills were tied to his belt. His chest was bare to the cold night air. Thrown over one shoulder was a robe of soft beaver skins. His silver-trimmed moccasins shone on the frosty ground.

"Forgive small joke I play you," Silverheels said. "Could not hold back when I saw *meaneleneh,* young man, drop from window and creep around side to surprise imaginary foe. Foe would be very stupid to walk bridge to guarded mill, yes? You think Silverheels that stupid? No, first he make sure only his friend is here."

Winthrop studied Silverheels' face in the moonlight. The half-breed was pleased with himself. His face hinted

196

too that he had yet another surprise, one that made his chill blue eyes glint with excitement.

Hope trembled in Winthrop's question. "You have news of Father?"

Silverheels bowed slightly. "Silverheels has kept his promise. Has found the brave little man."

Winthrop saw in his mind's eye the small, gallant figure, the dark face, mild and yet strong. The months of anxiety and longing—his, Suzanne's, and Merry's—were swept away on the tide of joy rising in his heart. "Where?" Winthrop managed to ask.

"Is captive of small Delaware party on way to Chief Captain Pipes' town. Tomorrow they torture and burn your father at stake there."

Bewilderment and rage wrenched a cry from Winthrop. "You tell me this now?"

Silverheels lifted one hand. "Is the Indian way to tell facts, then explain. There is yet time. Come."

Winthrop began jerkily to load his musket.

"Leave gun here," Silverheels said flatly. "Will only be in way."

Winthrop stared at Silverheels, a flicker of suspicion in his dark eyes. Then he slowly dropped the musket under Silverheels' grim scrutiny.

"You have *manese,* a knife?" asked Silverheels.

Winthrop's hand crept to his hunting shirt. "A sharp one," he said, not caring that Silverheels might read into his tone a warning that he was on guard against any treachery.

Silverheels grunted and without another word made his way into the moonlit clearing, across the footbridge, and into the somber cedars along the rocky ledge of the creek.

Winthrop caught up with him as he entered a small open meadow. "Wait!" He jerked at Silverheels' robe. Silverheels stopped and turned, his face tight with anger.

"Where is the Delaware camp?" Winthrop demanded. "How far?"

Silverheels hesitated before he answered coldly. "To the north and west as far as you can walk before *Tepethkakesathwa*, tonight's moon, wanes."

Winthrop let out a breath. "One more question," he said "Why have the Delawares waited all this time to—" He was unable to go on.

"Kill little man?" Silverheels shrugged. "Delawares are inferior tribe, fools." His eyes lowered to Winthrop's hands, knotted into trembling fists. "White men sometimes fools too. Hasty in thoughts."

Winthrop forced himself to put on an air of calm.

"Delawares inferior because they believe everything they see," Silverheels went on, after the pause, while over his face passed a look of scorn. "They believe your father British trader, friend, because on him they find papers that say so. Two days ago real British trader come from Fort Niagara who prove papers not your father's, that he not friend to Delawares."

Winthrop took one startled look in to Silverheels' face and knew he spoke the truth. Swiftly he tried to put the pieces of the puzzle together. Josiah taken captive from Silverheels' hut by the Delaware but spared because they believed him to be a friendly British trader. That fit in with the intelligence St. Clair had received of a white man among the Delawares; with the chief at the Harmar treaty insisting, upon the interpreter's questioning, that the man was a British trader, not a captive. It fit in too with Suzanne's intuition that the man could be their father. Still, where did the papers Josiah must have carried come from? And why had he kept up the masquerade for so many months?

"Already we waste much time. Follow," Silverheels commanded.

The dark forest closed over them. Before he had gone half a mile Winthrop knew he would have to give up for a while attempting to find an answer to the riddle. Half attention was not enough if he was to keep up with Silverheels' swift, silent progress through the night. Only here and there did the moon's rays penetrate the tangled tree tops to show the winding trail Silverheels was making toward a ridge outlined against the sky. Winthrop held his head high trying to keep Silverheels in sight and pushed on, stumbling into small ravines and out again, slipping on loose rocks, floundering through briars, pushing aside matted vines, struggling upward.

Halfway to the summit of the ridge Silverheels halted and knelt by a spring that welled from an outcropping of moss-covered rocks. Winthrop dropped by his side and drank deeply, aware for the first time that he was sweating, although the night was bitterly cold. Silverheels sat back on his haunches and waited for Winthrop to drink his fill before he spoke. "Only yesterday on the mound I heard the little Firehead playing the box that makes music. She look sad when I come, say she expecting her Papa. I tell her he is found, to go tell you to come. I wait. No one comes."

"Then how——" Winthrop leaned forward breathlessly.

"No one comes, so I go. Very cautious. The place bristle with guns. Silverheels know soldiers either laugh at him or shoot him so I slip through outer stockade and listen at back window of house. Little Firehead have had bad fall." Silver-heels tapped his head. "People think she talk crazy. So I learn where you are." Silverheels placed his hands palm down on the ground, a sign that he had finished.

Winthrop fought for composure. One word wrong, one false gesture, he knew, and Silverheels would indeed be finished. Probably he had talked this night more than he was accustomed to in a month. But Winthrop had to know about Merry. "Apetotha?" he asked softly in Shawnee.

"*Neeshematha,* my little sister, sleep with peace. When she wake, be well." Silverheels rose abruptly and looked at the moon. "We waste much time in talk," he muttered, and started off at a trot.

Winthrop stood up, but before he took a step, forced himself into an inflexible calmness. He must have only one thought, to get as quickly as possible to the Delaware camp where his father was prisoner. He felt for the knife in his hunting shirt. He would need everything he could reserve for whatever awaited him there. He began once more to follow Silverheels, ploddingly now. As the night wore on, he lost track of time and distance. They might have gone four miles or eight, and he could not guess how many more miles lay between him and the Delaware camp. "As far as you can walk before the moon wanes," Silverheels had said. Had it begun a slight downward arc in the night sky?

They journeyed on, Silverheels setting a rapid pace

along the ridge, crossing through a deep glen to another wooded hill top, and still another. By now Winthrop's dogged calmness was shaken. He began to wonder if the Delawares had broken camp and were already on the march toward Captain Pipes' town. Or if the warriors in a fit of impatience had already begun their terrible work on Josiah. He lengthened his stride in a sudden fever of desperation and came to Silverheels' side.

Silverheels stopped, his shrewd glance seeing Winthrop's misery. "Like *Meshepeshe,* the panther, look well now before you spring," Silverheels said softly, pointing downward to where the Muskingum made a shining rift through the deep-shadowed valley. Winthrop's eyes dropped to the distance below and he stared wildly over the landscape, searching for whatever it was Silverheels wanted him to see. Then his gaze fastened on a pinpoint of light in the gloom beyond the river. Was it—yes—a campfire! Somewhere near it was his father.

Winthrop's heart raced with excitement as they made their downward way. Then a new sort of calmness came over him, the light, eager poise of the marksman taking final aim. He followed Silverheels silently on his winding trail along the forest slope, into and out of a pine grove, and through a hazel thicket that dwindled and ended abruptly at the margin of a meadow. Silverheels dropped to his stomach and worked his way into the tall grass with an easy slithering movement. "Is good caution to go from here like *Shemenetoo,* the snake." When Winthrop joined him, Silverheels stood waiting, his eyes gleaming with a savage joy in the shadows of the willows at the river's edge.

"Once more we talk, then that is all. Listen well. I have hid canoe here. We cross in silence when *Pasquahe,* the cloud, covers moon."

Winthrop looked skyward, saw the big cloud slowly drifting, edged now with silver as it neared the full moon.

"Camp is beyond willows. I wait at water's edge for you to return." He glared down at Winthrop. "Silverheels is not coward, but farther he will not go."

Winthrop understood, and through his admiration felt a stab of pity for the lonely man whose loyalties would always be divided.

The dark cloud drifted over the moon and the shadows deepened. *"Mishemenetoc,* the Good Spirit, be with you!" Silverheels said, and dropped into the birchbark canoe. Winthrop stepped in and knelt at the prow. With long feathering strokes that left scarcely a ripple they worked their way across the silent river. Soundlessly Silverheels guided the canoe under an overhanging willow and drove his paddle into the mud bank. Winthrop looked back. Silverheels sat straight and expressionless, staring ahead.

On hands and knees Winthrop crawled up the bank. At the top he paused long enough to plan his way through the maze of willows. The soil was sandy and could be treacherous where it had drifted over roots and stones. He crept on with the utmost caution toward the end of the grove where light from the campfire penetrated and flickered fitfully. Nearer and nearer he went until the light made an orange glow on his hands. Then he circled to the dark side of the grove, stood up, and looked into the Indian camp.

A score of Delawares slept on the ground in their

blankets near the fire. Hunters and warriors. In a hurry. Hadn't taken time to build shelter. Traveling without women, children, or dogs. But where was Josiah? Winthrop looked wildly about the small clearing. There, at the edge of the grove, about where he had circled back from the firelight! A figure lying across and bound to a bowed sapling! Nearby an Indian hunched in his fur robe. His ornaments showed he was an honored veteran of many battles. Winthrop's eyes went again to the small motionless figure, uncovered to the cold night. He had a sudden qualm of despair that cleared as he saw Josiah's arms move slightly.

Winthrop drew a deep breath and began to retrace his path, hoping the wind in the willows was louder than the pounding of his heart. He inched along on his stomach, halting several times to move twigs or leaves from the ground ahead of him. Finally he came up without a sound behind the bowed sapling. Luck was with him. The Indian guard was dozing. Winthrop let his gaze drop now to Josiah who lay bound to the young tree, his head turned away from the firelight. Little did Josiah resemble the sober miller Winthrop remembered. Mud-clotted buckskin replaced the homespun. The black hair which had always been worn tied neatly back was a loose tangle. Josiah's hands—Winthrop choked back a cry of outrage as he saw them—swollen, torn, the wrists bleeding under the tight bonds. It was evident that he had tried for hours to work them free of the rawhide and had given up.

Winthrop drew his knife and crept into the circle of firelight to Josiah's side. With a trembling finger he touched Josiah on the shoulder, adding a pressure of warning. Josiah's head slowly turned, and after the long months Winthrop saw again his father's face. It had not changed. The same quiet strength was there, though from it hope had gone. Now as Josiah's gaze met Winthrop's, hope leaped to life again. Winthrop moved quickly to cut the deerhide thongs, but the warning in Josiah's eyes was quicker.

Knife poised, Winthrop followed Josiah's intent stare to the tip of the sapling where it was pegged to the ground. Tied to the foremost branch was a cowbell. At another point halfway up the tree's length was tied another, and another! So that was why the guard dozed, why Josiah had lain so still. An unusual movement would have set up a clangor sufficient to bring every warrior from slumber to his feet.

Warily Winthrop slipped his hand over the clapper, cut loose the first cowbell and laid it slowly, carefully, on the ground; then the second, and the last. When he bent to cut Josiah loose, his hands were slippery with sweat. Keeping an eye on the guard, Josiah rose while Winthrop held down the sapling. Then together they gripped the tree and eased it upright.

Winthrop pointed silently to the river, then turned and ducked for the cover of the thicket. He could hear Josiah behind him, slipping over roots, blundering into low-hanging branches. From the clearing rose the clang of a cowbell and an angry shout. It was too late to be cautious. "Run for it!" He reached a hand back to his father and half led, half dragged him through the willows and over the slippery bank.

"Here!" a voice whispered.

Winthrop and Josiah dropped into the canoe and seized the paddles Silverheels thrust at them. They paddled furious-

Warily, Winthrop cut loose the first cowbell

ly until they reached the deep shadows of the opposite shore-line, before they paused to look back. Torches streaked like fireflies through the darkness as the warriors ran about in howling confusion to pick up the trail they could not find. Silverheels' smile of satisfaction curled into a grimace of disdain. "I tell you, Delawares fools. They do not think to look in river, yet. We journey on fast with current before they do."

There was no time for talk until almost an hour later when Silverheels pointed to a cluster of cabins in the moonlight on the eastern shore. "Plainfield. Your brothers, *English-manake,* await you there." He dug his paddle deep into the river and guided the canoe toward a small beach a rod above the landing.

"They will have a real welcome for their brother Silverheels, too," Josiah said.

Silverheels eased the prow of the canoe onto the beach. "Silverheels have no blood brothers." He sat very straight in the bow of the canoe and motioned for Josiah and Winthrop to get out.

"You have to come, Silverheels," Winthrop insisted. "After all you've done for us, and we haven't had a chance to thank you, or anything." He faltered under Silverheels' steady gaze.

"Boy must learn that he does favor to Silverheels when he allows him to be useful. This night I have used the skills and cunning that once make Silverheels great. Have outwitted *Matche-le-ne-tha-tha,* my old enemies. Is enough."

Josiah turned and clasped Silverheels' hand and looked long into his face. The gratitude Silverheels would not hear was there for him to see. "Until another day, then," Josiah said, and stepped out of the canoe.

"When the day of trouble ends between brothers," Silverheels said in his soft voice. He looked up at Winthrop, who stood watching him with a melancholy expression, and a twinkle of amusement shone in Silverheels' blue eyes. "Is promise. This time do not doubt."

Winthrop's arrival with his father wakened the small new settlement. First one candle, then another, blinked on as the news went from door to door. Soon firelight, too, glowed from every window. Men rumpled with sleep came running into the clearing, pressing them with questions.

"Please, a little later," Josiah said, smiling.

"The man's had a rough time of it," a bearded one with his woolen breeches pulled over his nightshirt said gruffly, noticing Josiah's hands. "Let him be until he's got his second wind." He turned toward a cabin at the edge of the clearing and called, "Boil some water!" In a few minutes a woman ran by with a kettle of steaming water, a comb, and clean folded linen. A young man about Winthrop's age came up and touched him shyly on the shoulder. "Ma's put venison on the fire."

It was warm inside the cabin where the woman moved softly about the fireplace. The young man motioned for Winthrop to take a chair at the trestle table, then sat in the corner and stared at him with a look of awe. When Winthrop lifted the steaming mug set before him his hands began to tremble so that he spilled some of the liquid. The woman looked up and smiled. "You are weary. You will sleep?" She motioned toward a feather tick in the corner.

Josiah answered for him from the doorway. "Not yet, good madam." He stood there freshly bathed, the mud brushed from his buckskins, hair still wet from the comb. A look of peace and joy shone from his dark eyes. "There is word I must carry to Campus Martius." His voice lowered. "And it has been long since I have seen my daughters." He looked inquiringly at Winthrop. "Our friends have made us the loan of two saddle horses."

Winthrop rose, fatigue falling from him like a worn cloak at the sight of his father's face.

"I'm ready."

CHAPTER SIXTEEN

"If we ride hard we should reach Campus Martius by dawn," Winthrop turned in the saddle to tell his father, after they had said their farewells to the kindly people of Plainfield and started along the woodland trail.

"I see you have learned your way about," Josiah said, appraising Winthrop with a glance that took in the deepened chest, the widened shoulders, and the confident lift of his head.

Winthrop flushed with pleasure, but the glowing account he had planned to give of his work with the surveyors and the construction crew dwindled to one word. "Some."

They cantered a while in silent companionship that had a new element, strange, yet secure.

"What happened?" Winthrop asked finally, reining in his horse.

Josiah came abreast of Winthrop and they rode side by side on the narrow trail. "I asked myself that same question while I lay bound to the sapling." Josiah spoke slowly, groping toward a truth almost within his grasp. "Sometimes a force bigger than ourselves catches us up and sweeps us along with it. Remember the song your mother used to sing? 'The seed is blown before the wind'?"

Winthrop stole a glance at his father and saw that the look of grief had been smoothed and eased by time. "We'll

Josiah came abreast of Winthrop

never forget," he answered simply. Both were lost for a moment in their own reverie.

"Silverheels told me the Delawares thought you were a British trader friendly to their tribe," Winthrop said, directing Josiah's mind again to his question.

"Yes." Josiah sighed. "I do not blame the warriors for planning to burn me at the stake when they found out that I had deceived them. Nor do I particularly blame the British agent for exposing me. The information I had gathered could do great harm to British plans to strengthen the grip they have never loosed on the Northwest Territory." He paused, then added thoughtfully, "This new world is a strange place where the people worthy and capable of being our friends must become our enemies. Believe me, although spying is necessary, it is a sad game."

"Spying?" Winthrop asked in astonishment.

"An odd occupation for a peaceable miller! But that is part of what I was trying to tell you—how one can get caught up in something bigger than himself, and be swept along with it."

"Back at Plainfield you said you had a message to carry to Campus Martius?"

Josiah smiled ruefully. "I did have quite a report before the warriors burned it to ashes! What remains I carry in my head." His tone told Winthrop to ask no more.

Winthrop's obedient but questioning glance was not lost on his father. "It all goes back to that July day on the Ohio," Josiah continued. "Just before the arrow hit me, I picked up a packet fallen from the dead trader's pocket, expecting later to write to his kin."

"Trader?" Winthrop asked in surprise. "I thought the men were trappers by the look of them." Then he grinned. "Silverheels would say, 'White men sometimes fools. Believe everything they see.'"

"The packet was still with me, unopened, when the Delawares took me from Silverheels' lodge. Later when I opened it and saw the identification papers of a British trader I used them as a sort of shield, knowing the bond of friendship between the Indians and the British. I planned to keep up the pose until I was strong enough to leave and make my way back to you."

"Then you got in it too thick to leave?"

"Yes, though I was daily watching for a chance to get away without arousing suspicion."

"And the British agent came—"

"Then you came," Josiah said with a smile, "and here we are." Plainly he did not want to talk of his ordeal under the hands of the warriors. "Now, enough of my affairs. Tell me what has happened with you. All of it, from the day we parted on the river."

"Yes, Father." The words released a tide of memories. The months behind Winthrop took on a meaning they had lacked, a pattern leading to this early dawn. When he brought his story to the present they had passed the huge sycamore that marked the place where the trail cut back from the river into the hills.

Josiah repeated the names that had been often mentioned in Winthrop's recital. "Mrs. McKnight, Anselm Tupper, John Matthews, the Dutch corporal, Peter Nyswonger, General Putnam, Governor St. Clair, Silverheels

— most of the names are strange, but the people are no longer strangers to me."

Winthrop himself had not known the people of the colony had come to play so great a role in his life. The realization of it kindled other enthusiasms he wanted to share with his father. He spoke of the Ohio in spring, swarming with passing flatboats; of the Muskingum cool and green and quiet in summer at the farthest reaches of the surveys; of the fertile bottomlands, the forest hills, of Wolf Creek Mills not far from Plainfield, of the Donation Tract.

"It will go hard with you to leave?"

Winthrop swallowed. "I hadn't thought that far."

Josiah glanced shrewdly at Winthrop in the growing light. "Is there need to think further?" he asked, and without waiting went on, "Tell me more of the children."

"Suzanne isn't exactly a child," Winthrop began, pensively. "Or maybe it's that she's taken to wearing her hair up like the ladies. Or that Mrs. McKnight has taught her to do the things womenfolk do about a household. She does them right well, too, when she isn't daydreaming."

"I must stop thinking of her as a child," Josiah murmured. "At her age, a year and a half, nearly, is a bridge from childhood to young womanhood. I regret I could not walk it with her."

"I think Anselm Tupper stands at the far end with outstretched hand." Winthrop smiled, a little sadly.

"So? Then she has grown away from me entirely."

"No." Winthrop spoke positively. "Never Suzanne."

"Merry used to fit just into the crook of my arm," Josiah said hungrily.

"She is the pet of Campus Martius. Only Mrs. Mc-Knight's soundness has kept us all from spoiling her."

"She can't be too grown up," Josiah ventured hopefully. "Only a small child would be so carefree as to wander alone into the woods, these dangerous times, playing a music box."

"She told Silverheels she was expecting you," Winthrop said. "The song would bring you—sing you home." He kept looking straight ahead as he heard his father's sharply in-drawn breath.

The trail took a sudden turn upward. Winthrop, knowing their journey was near its end, urged his horse on-ward. As he drew up at the hilltop, Josiah reined in beside him.

"Here we are," Winthrop said, standing in the stirrups and looking down upon the settlement.

Josiah stared silently at the scene. The wooded hillside sloped sharply away to a more gradual descent where only the stumps of trees remained, and leveled to a plain over which the moundbuilders' earthworks set a strange geo-metric pattern. In the midst of them rose Campus Martius, its towers pricking upward, tinted with the dawn light. Be-yond, the Muskingum curved under the shelter of the forest ridge to meet the Ohio. Fort Harmar and the stockaded Point stood like sentinels at opposite sides of the river mouth, guarding the gateway to the Northwest. Far across the wide Ohio with its long crescent-shaped island, lay Isaac Williams' huddled settlement, and in the distant east loomed the blue hills of Virginia crested with the streaming gold and scarlet banners of sunrise.

The man drew a deep breath of admiration. "No wonder!" he exclaimed. "No wonder President Washington looks with such favor and concern on this land. It's worth putting up a fight for. Come," he said abruptly, "direct me to the guardhouse."

Winthrop turned his horse into the stony path that branched downward from the trail. They cut through the woodland in back of the cone-shaped mound, past the pest houses still standing on the plain, across the cornfield, and galloped onto the main road to Campus Martius. As they drew to the gate, the flag rose briskly above the belfry tower. At almost the same moment the air was stirred with the throaty ga-boom of Fort Harmar's small cannon greeting the rising sun.

Winthrop swung from the saddle and took the bridle of Josiah's horse. "I'll tend the mounts," he said, knowing Josiah must deliver his message alone. "I'll wait."

"You'll not have long to wait this time." Josiah's smile flashed in his dark weary face. He spoke a word to the guard, who swung the gate open for him, went into the square, and rapped smartly at the guardhouse door.

"Who calls?" asked a soldierly voice.

Josiah paused, savoring the moment for which he had long waited. For the first time in many months, he spoke his own name. "Josiah Lake. I would speak with your post major, Anselm Tupper, on urgent business."

Anselm received him alone in the small bare room. They clasped hands for a moment in silence, each taking the other's measure in the way of men.

"Welcome, sir," Anselm said gravely. "The sentinel announced a stranger approaching with Winthrop." He paused. "But you are certainly not an outsider to us. Everyone from the Governor to the youngest private has been looking for you." His eyes dropped to Josiah's wrists. "Except for the tell-tale marks of your bonds you appear little worse for your escape."

"Rescue," Josiah corrected Anselm's word. "It was Winthrop's doing. And Silverheels'. But more of that later." He looked into the square, his gaze searching the blank windows and rows of closed doors. "Forgive me if I seem hurried."

"I am the one to ask your pardon," Anselm said. "Your charge must indeed be urgent if it brings you here before a reunion with your daughters."

Josiah nodded in silence. Then he said bluntly, "During the months I was in the wilderness I passed some time tallying the strength of the various tribes and of the British soldiers who are allied against us."

Anselm's eyebrows went up in surprise, but his manner changed at once from the personal to the alert attention of the man of military training. "Shall I summon Governor St. Clair and General Putnam at once, sir?"

Josiah ran his hand impatiently over his hair. "The figures I had written are now in ashes. I'd like time to prepare a formal report before I face such a personage as the Governor."

"I understand," Anselm agreed. He drew back a chair for Josiah and sat across the desk from him, waiting.

"It is common knowledge that the British are not yet ready to give up their posts as they had agreed to do at the conclusion of the late war. It is also known that they encourage the Indians to ignore similarly the treaties that some of the tribes have signed at Fort Stanwix and at Fort Harmar. Encouraging means actually furnishing them with free supplies and arms and ammunition to use against us."

Anselm whistled softly. "General Putnam has had reason, then, to order the tightening of our defenses."

"Certainly these facts are known to your leaders." Josiah hitched his chair forward and leaned across the table, "But, I wonder, do they know that besides the Indians and the British, we may have a third nation to fight?"

"Who?" Anselm asked incredulously.

"Spain."

"No!" the young post major exclaimed, the look of astonishment spreading on his face.

"There is a movement afoot to form an alliance of British, Indian, and Spanish forces to dislodge the settlers along the Ohio."

"Why?"

"Because our boats are demanding free access to the sea, and Spain fears she will lose control of the Mississippi Valley. Greed, Major Tupper. Greed that made the British take fur, valued at one hundred thousand dollars, from our territory into Canada last year. Greed that is using the Indians as pawns."

Anselm rose, and his fingers drummed nervously upon the table. "This is news of importance far beyond me as a mere post major."

Josiah sighed. "And beyond me as a humble miller. But until the morrow when I shall report more fully, I'll consider my duty discharged."

Anselm squared his shoulder. "You have done a great service. It is not fitting that a soldier of my low stature should be the first one to congratulate you, but as one person to another—" He held out his hand.

"Thank you," said Josiah.

Anselm walked with him to the door and pointed across the square. "Mrs. McKnight's is always the first chimney to billow with the smoke of the breakfast fire. And by the way, you may tell her she need not worry about having to move. At the evening's directors' meeting, it was voted to give her a hundred-acre donation lot partly in recognition of her many services to the families at Campus Martius and partly because her late husband, had he not lost his life at the Falls of the Muskingum attack, would be eligible for such a tract."

Josiah looked at the fat chimney, and at its plume of homey smoke. "What reward is great enough for one who has more than befriended his children?" he mused.

"Another thing," Anselm remembered. "Rufus Putnam has a draft made out to you for the meal Winthrop and Suzanne offered the settlement during the famine. We hope you may see fit to turn it back into our company and become one of us. That alone would reward Mrs. McKnight. It would go hard with her—with all of us—if you should carry our young charges off to Kentucky."

Josiah turned in the doorway. "That is a family matter that will take some discussion. Would you care to call this evening?"

Anselm looked searchingly at Josiah; a smile grew and deepened in his gray eyes. "I'll be there," he said emphatically.

The color bearers wheeled and marched across the drill ground toward the guardhouse. "One more question," Anselm said, putting out a hand to detain Josiah. "Is Campus Martius in immediate danger?"

"The Indians have a healthy fear of the guns of Fort Harmar, the Point, and Campus Martius, and a respect for your scouting system. In general, your people have treated the tribes fairly. The attacks will probably be against less defensible outposts."

Winthrop, having arranged for the care of their borrowed horses, caught up with Josiah as he hurried across the square. When the man hesitated at Mrs. McKnight's doorway, Winthrop whispered, "Go ahead, knock!" and stepped aside.

Josiah first tapped the door lightly; then he rapped soundly.

From inside came the sound of much fussing with bolts and bars before the door opened a crack. A suspicious brown eye peered at Josiah.

"La!" Mrs. McKnight cried. "This is no time to come pounding on people's doors." She narrowed the crack. "If you are the gentleman from Boston that's come to take over these quarters, please go away. Return at a proper hour of the morning and we'll be moved out bag and baggage."

Josiah's laugh rang out. "Open up, Mistress McKnight! I bring you word that you have been awarded a hundred-acre lot! You no longer have need of these quarters."

"What kind of prank is this? Go away before you waken the child."

Winthrop stepped forward. "We've come for breakfast. This is my father, Master Josiah Lake, miller," he announced proudly.

Mrs. McKnight's glance sharpened. "You—you're Josiah Lake, the children's father?"

"I am." Josiah bowed.

"It really is, at last," Winthrop said, his smile glowing.

The woman turned her gaze slowly from one to the other. Then her eyes rested on Josiah's face. Her expression changed from doubt to a swift gleam of recognition that broadened to a smile of welcome. She opened the door wide and turned to call in a breathless voice, "Suzanne!"

Suzanne hurried from the back room, folding a quilt as she came. The quilt spilled to the floor as Josiah strode in. "Father! You've come!" She ran toward him and stopped short, surprised that she no longer had to reach up to the outstretched arms. Then her bright head was against his dark one. "Merry was right!" she cried.

Josiah stepped back and looked at Suzanne. "So?" He touched the fair braids pinned high on her head. "But still not too big for this?" He lifted her slowly and held her aloft.

"Never!" Suzanne smiled radiantly.

Josiah's eyes searched the long narrow room.

"Merry's asleep in the back room," Suzanne told him softly.

Josiah went in alone. He sat quietly on the edge of the bunk where Merry lay. He moved the fringe of his soiled buckskin jacket aside so that it would not touch her. Her face had lost its baby look now, he saw, but it had taken on even more of the elfin beauty of her mother's. Once he put out his hand as if to wake her, then drew it back. If

220

He touched the fair braids pinned high on her head

she should waken now it might startle her; then he could not look at her this way as long as he pleased.

After a while he rejoined the rest who waited for him at the fireplace. "Ah, Mrs. McKnight." He smiled, as she pushed a chair near the blaze for him. "A civilized indoor fire with ovens for baking stone bread!"

"Take care lest you scorch," she said, and the smiles ran out over the little wrinkle paths at the corners of her eyes. She bent to mop up the mush that had boiled over onto the hearth. "All this time, and you should find the house looking like this!"

"I am honored to be admitted," Josiah said, with a half teasing glance.

"My!" Mrs. McKnight's capable hands fluttered to brush an imaginary crumb from the table. "How I must have sounded! For days I've been expecting a gentleman from Boston to come and turn us out."

"Winthrop has told me," Josiah said gravely. "However, it should not be hard to leave two rooms when one has one hundred acres waiting."

Her eyes darted from Winthrop to Josiah. "Then it was not a prank? I have been given a donation lot?"

"Indeed, yes, if Anselm Tupper's word is good—"

"Oh, it is!" Suzanne exclaimed, rising. Then she sank back in the shadows to hide her blushing face.

"Well," Josiah said, as he stared into the fire, "that leaves the Lakes to be disposed of. Winthrop, what have you to say?"

"We still have the Kentucky boat," Winthrop offered uncertainly.

"So we have," Josiah agreed.

Winthrop looked disappointed.

"We have also a draft against the meal you sold and an invitation to turn it back into the Ohio Company and become one of the associates," Josiah continued.

Winthrop leaped to his feet. "Father, we need a good miller here. I'm nearly old enough to lay claim to a section of the donation lands. There's a place in the hills I want you to see—"

"Not so fast!" Josiah interrupted. "Suzanne?"

Suzanne looked at Mrs. McKnight and answered without hesitation. "Some people here have come to mean more than friends to me."

"Mrs. McKnight?" Josiah inquired, his gratitude shining in his eyes. "You're the only land holder among us, so you should have two votes."

Mrs. McKnight found her voice. "Voting is for men-folks." Her eyes twinkled. "So is farming. Winthrop would be a good neighbor to have when my fence needs mending or my wood cording."

"We'll still go on to Kentucky, though, if you want us to, Father," Winthrop said, anxiously.

There was a long silence while Josiah stared again into the fire. He rose abruptly, went to the back room and, holding Merry, still asleep, returned to his chair by the fire. Merry was not too big to fit into the crook of his arm. "Now we're all here," Josiah said.

Suzanne got the music box and turned the handle.

A look came over Josiah's face as if someone had touched it softly. "Now we're all here," he repeated.

Merry woke and smiled drowsily. "You did come home, didn't you, Papa? Silverheels promised."

"Yes," Josiah answered, "I've come home."

Although unrest and rumor of warfare seethed through the wilderness, here inside Campus Martius was a small, secure block of peace; here was rest.

Merry sighed and settled deeper into the crook of Josiah's arm. "Sing the song. Sing all of it."

While Suzanne played the tune, Josiah sang.

> *The seed is blown before the wind*
> *And where it comes to rest,*
> *Be it on mountain meadow green*
> *Or river's edge where willows lean—*

The last two lines that had slipped down out of Winthrop's memory came back to him and he joined in lustily.

> *There is the land with beauty blest;*
> *There is the home my spirit quests.*

"That's it," Merry murmured happily.

Each, in his own way, silently agreed.

PRINTED IN U.S.A.

Date Due

JY 23 '70					
Fac.					
AP 10 '72					
NO 20 '73					
AP 7 '74					

O. 23231

54256

J
W

54256

J
W

Wright, Alice
    The seed is blown.